Charlie James

FISH

BLOOMSBURY

First published in Great Britain in 2006 by Bloomsbury Publishing Plc
36 Soho Square, London, W1D 3QY

A CIP catalogue record of this book is available from the British Library

ISBN 978 0 7475 7976 2

All papers used by Bloomsbury Publishing are natural, recyclable
products made from wood grown in well-managed forests. The
manufacturing processes conform to the environmental regulations of
the country of origin.

Typeset by Dorchester Typesetting Group Ltd
Printed in Great Britain by Clays Ltd, St Ives Plc

5 7 9 10 8 6 4

www.bloomsbury.com

For Mark, Charlotte and James

Contents

PROLOGUE

I hate fish.

They are slippery. They are scaly. And, let's face it, they stink.

So when my brother turned into a cod, I was, quite frankly, disgusted.

I mean, a *cod*? Have you seen what they look like? They are ugly and flabby and they taste like cardboard – especially when served under a thick white sauce with green specks. Mum calls it Parsley Sauce. I call it Seaweed Sludge.

I ask you, if he was going to turn into a fish, couldn't the idiot have turned into something slightly more exciting?

Couldn't he at least have been – well, a *shark*?

Chapter 1

BILL IS BORED

I blame Bill.

I reckon it was all his fault. Of course, he doesn't agree with me. He swears it was all an accident and that he didn't mean to do anything wrong.

Didn't mean to do anything wrong? Well, excuse me for breathing, but who does he think he is? I mean, can we just take a quick reality check?

Here's a list.

THINGS I HAD TO DO FOR BILL (BUT RATHER WISH I HADN'T)

1. Rescue him from the jaws of death, not once – but twice.

2. Square up to the local bully.
3. Risk total and utter social humiliation in front of the whole school.

You see? And all because of the things Bill did which he shouldn't have done. Get the picture? That boy is nuts.

Bill is my younger brother. He is six years old and has fair hair, blue eyes and a tendency for nits. Those who don't know him think he looks like an angel – but if Bill's an angel, heaven has a problem. It's not that Bill is nasty or anything like that. It's just that, well, Bill is Trouble – Trouble with a capital T. Whatever he does, wherever he goes, Trouble follows, particularly when Bill is bored. And on this particular day, Bill was *particularly* bored …

It was Saturday. Dad was out, Mum was in the garden and Stacey (my sister) was in her bedroom painting her nails a disgusting shade of blue. As for me, I was lying in bed pretending to be ill. Now before you think I'm completely sad, there was a reason – though it is dead embarrassing and I can hardly bring myself to write the truth. You see, I was – *ahem* – swotting for the Inter-School Quiz

Championship and I didn't want anyone – least of all my parents – to know.

Let me try to explain …

The Inter-School Quiz Championship is held once every three years. It is a huge event and schools from all round the town compete to win the mega first prize. And this year it was immense – a brand, spanking new TOL3 complete with the latest PlayStation, wide-screen TV and surround-sound cinema. Sound good? You bet! Look good? Even better!

There was only one tiny little problem with my plan – me. I can never remember a single fact, however hard I try; unlike my younger brother, who was born with the best memory I've ever come across. I read all the books and look at all the information. But looking is as far as it goes. It's in one eye and out the other. As soon as anyone asks me anything, I start to panic. My face turns red, my palms grease up and I look like a halibut on toast (or so Stacey kindly tells me). It's totally gross. But by then, I was too desperate to care. I was ready to risk everything to win that prize.

And if you're wondering why I didn't ask my

parents for help – well, the answer's simple: it's because of PDS (Parental Disapproval Syndrome). They simply Don't Approve of PlayStations, or TVs or computers or anything that's at all necessary or important to life. Forget about TOL3s, all they want us to do is eat our five portions of fruit and veg and play outside. Honestly, it's so unfair. I'm sure it's against our human rights or something. Just to prove my point, here are the (completely idiotic) reasons why I reckon we are the only family in the street not to have a PlayStation, let alone any gadgets that don't pre-date the Black Death:

Dad: *'A PlayStation/TOL3 is not a fish.'*

I know, I know. This is a difficult one to get your head round, but if you can just bear with me for a few more pages, I'll try and explain.

Mum: *'A PlayStation/TOL3 is not organic, educational, powered by fresh air or attached to a ball of wool.'*

Mum is nuts on knitting.

Stacey: *'A PlayStation/TOL3 is not a boy/ make-up/hair gel/an item of clothing/a mobile phone accessory etc etc.'*

Welcome to Planet Stacey.

And wow, are our parents stubborn. Bill and I have tried and tried to change their minds at least a hundred zillion times. We even offered to make our beds in the morning (well, once a week at least). But each time they trot out the same, tired excuses:

Mum (to Bill): *'Whaddya-need-a-computer/TOL3/ PlayStation-for-when-you-could-play-outside-in-the-fresh-air-instead-of-being-cooped-up-inside-all-day-staring-at-a-screen?'*

It was Christmas.
It was snowing.
I rest my case.

Dad (to me). '*In my days-boys-had-to-amuse-themselves-and-make-their-own-toys, chairs, tables, beds …!*' Oops! Slight exaggeration there, sorry, it just slipped in … Back to Dad.

'*And-anyway-don't-you-think-you-should-be-studying-your-maths-and-have-you-done-your-homework-yet?*'

See what I mean? I don't think he understands the concept of free time.

As for Stacey … Well, I am sure she would help us if she could get her brain into gear. She used to be really fun, but all she does now is read magazines and sigh – a lot! Bill thinks her brain's gone soft from washing her hair twice a day, but I think girls are just *weird*.

Anyway – back to 'Boring' Saturday and why my

brother was in such a strop. Bill was bored because Mum and Dad were busy, Stacey wouldn't give him the time of day and I ... well, I was lying in a darkened room with a towel wrapped round my head, like a true saddo, trying to revise. And the worst of it was, I couldn't tell anyone my plan. My parents would have bent my ear about how I was doing for the wrong reasons (you know the sort of thing):

(Dad): *'Education is an end in itself!'*
(Mum): *'You shouldn't need bribes to work hard!'*

Even supposing I *did* win, I bet they'd have made me promise to give the stuff away so that they could replace it with an Educational Toy. Stacey wasn't interested and try as I might, I could not bring myself to tell Bill. Even supposing he could keep his mouth shut, it would raise his hopes and he would only get disappointed if I failed. So, no, I had to go it alone. This was my secret.

Though little did I know then that there was another secret-keeper in our family.

Which brings me neatly back to Saturday and Bill.

Chapter 2
BILL'S SECRET

Bill tried very hard to get me out of bed that morning. He knew I was faking it and was longing to know what was going on. But I just lay there groaning artistically and begging him – in a faint voice – not to draw the curtains as the light hurt my eyes. Even if I say it myself, it was an Oscar-winning performance.

When it was quite clear that I wasn't going to budge, he got into a right strop and stomped downstairs into the kitchen, looking for something to eat. Bill is permanently hungry. Unfortunately for him, since Mum's gone on her latest health kick, she's got rid of all the crisps, biscuits and chocolate bars and replaced them with dried fruit and carrot juice.

But, being Bill, he was in luck. At the back of a cupboard that took him a mere five minutes to ransack, he found the last packet of his favourite Monster Munch crisps – the ones in a bright purple packet with a picture of a pterodactyl being devoured by a tyrannosaurus rex. Bill loves crisps, and this flavour – pickled gherkin and tomato – was his favourite. They were history in a matter of nanoseconds.

After that his luck ran out.

Despite an intensive search, Bill could find nothing more worth eating. But he did notice a large and important-looking box on the kitchen table. It was addressed to Dad. On the top and on each side were large labels with red lettering:

FISH SAMPLES!

IMPORTANT!

TOP SECRET!

WARNING! For fish only!

DEFINITELY NOT FOR HUMAN CONSUMPTION!

To be fair to Bill, it was lying around for anyone to see.

But to be fair to us, anyone else in the family would have read the warning and left it alone.

Bill, though, is different. Bill (if you remember) was bored. Trouble was on its way.

He read the warning labels on the box. (Bill is seriously bright and can read just about as well as I can). He immediately went into Curious Mode and decided to explore some more.

Bill opened the box.

It was full of multicoloured packets labelled 'FISH CRISPS'. Inside, there was also a letter addressed to Dad. It wasn't in an envelope, so Bill decided it would be OK to read it. This is what it said:

Dear Mr Finn

Thank you for your box of Fish Crisps for Homes and Aquariums. We think they are the best fish crisps in the world!

Please send us enough to feed our killer whale – the one we have just rescued from a film set in Hollywood. She arrives at the zoo next week, along with our new Marine Life Manager, Ms Donna Mezzweme.

Yours sincerely
Eimer Boss
Director
Z.E.B.R.A. Zoos (Zoos for Endangered Beasts
and Rare Animals)

P.S. When we were testing your second set of samples —
Super-Strong Fish Crisps for Scarce Sea Fish — an expert
here swears he saw a fish change shape briefly. Is this
possible? Please do some more trials. The left-over packets
are in this box. Annoyingly, their labels have become
smudged with sea water.

P.P.S. Watch out! Guard your samples with care! We hear
that those canny crooks, The Underwater Underworld, are
out to sabotage your valuable work to restock the oceans with
fish. Their spies are everywhere! Do not let your Super-
Strong Fish Crisps for Scarce Sea Fish fall into the wrong
hands! The future of the marine world depends on you,
Mr Finn!

Bill read the letter twice. Some of the words were new to him, but he made sense of them the second time round. He blinked. *Hollywood? Fish changing shape? Spies?* What on earth was going on – and, more importantly, what was Dad up to? Until now, he'd always thought that Dad's fish food business was rather dull and boring. All that stuff about increased haddock velocity and falling herring densities made his eyes water. How could it suddenly be so exciting? Surely it was up to him to find out. He decided there and then to help Dad survive this murky underwater world – oh, and perhaps eat a few crisp samples on the way. After all, anything had to be better than dried fruit. So he quickly stuffed as many packets of fish crisps as he thought he could get away with into the pockets of his cargo pants, replaced the letter and carefully closed the box.

Then he sat down to work out what to do next.

And no one was even the teensiest, weeniest bit suspicious about what he had done.

Except for me.

Chapter 3
THE MYSTERIOUS BOX

FISH SAMPLES!
IMPORTANT!
TOP SECRET!
WARNING! For fish only!
DEFINITELY NOT FOR HUMAN CONSUMPTION!

It was lunchtime, and upstairs in my bedroom I was as hungry as Bill and twice as bored. I had been swotting away *for three hours* (well, two and a half if you count that short recreational break I took to reach the next level on Bill's Game Boy – a present from sympathetic Glam Gran). But it was no good. I couldn't remember a single thing. There was nothing for it but to stage the fastest recovery the world has ever seen. I drooped down to the kitchen to see what everyone was up to.

The first person I saw was Bill, who was lurking by the kitchen table, peering at a large box. He scowled at me – which I probably deserved – but I could tell he was up to something as soon as I saw his face. He was wearing that sort of shifty, I'm-up-to-no-good-and-I'm-not-going-to-let-on-what-it-is expression that I know only too well.

Just then, Mum bustled in from the garden and gave me a big hug. She was thrilled at my miraculous recovery and promised to make me a nice pot of boiled cod and tofu to keep my strength up. Personally, I would have preferred fried egg and chips, but as I could have eaten a table leg by that time, I nodded weakly and sat down next to Stacey, who had just appeared with the latest edition of her favourite magazine. She sniffed as though I was a bit of dog poo and looked away with a sigh.

Soon after that Dad waltzed into the kitchen, waving a large carrier bag in the air.

He tapped the box on the table, then tapped his nose as he surveyed his family with a beaming smile.

'Ah, yes,' he said happily, and almost to himself. 'I was expecting this delivery.'

There was a slight pause, and I noticed Bill watching Dad very closely. Dad, catching his eye, gave a quick start and seemed to pull himself together.

'Hello, Plankton! Hello, Sprats!' he said excitedly.

'Have I got something to show you! Just wait till you cod-a-load of what I have here. You'll be thrilled!' And he banged his bag down on the mysterious box.

We all sighed – well, all of us except Mum. Dad can do no wrong in her eyes. She thinks he's great. So do we, for that matter, but it's just that sometimes, Dad is so … *Dad*. You see, he's an inventor, a fish food manufacturer who is obsessed with fish: breeding them, feeding them, cooking them and eating them. It's his whole life, and the only thing – apart from us and Mum – that he's really interested in. Normally, I try to take an interest – it is his job, after all. But I had a gut feeling as I looked at this 'TOP SECRET!' box that this was going to be one plaice too far.

Mum, sweet as ever, clapped her hands with excitement. 'Oh, Dan!' she breathed. 'Is it more news about your fish food samples?'

'Yup!' said Dad, thumping his fist down on the box Bill had found. 'It is good, good news. This is it. I've finally done it. I've just invented the best fish food ever. Fish food that will get us noticed. Fish food that will make us rich! Fish food that will make –'

'Er, Dad,' I asked, interrupting him in mid-flow. If he went on uninterrupted, I might lose the will to live. 'Just tell us why it's so good?'

Dad coughed and looked a little furtive. Then to our amazement, he started to behave in the oddest way. Even for him. He scuttled round the room, checking behind doors and peering out of the window. Then he drew the curtains, turned on the kitchen taps and switched the radio on full blast.

Even Mum was puzzled. 'Dan,' she asked, 'what are you doing?'

'Ssh!' answered Dad, putting his finger to his lips. 'Walls have ears!' And then, turning off the light, he took a torch out of his coat pocket, beckoned us round the kitchen table and opened the box. The letter and the samples were still there. I noticed that Bill was standing very still, but even so, he seemed to rustle slightly if he moved. I looked at him suspiciously, but it was no good. Dad was holding the torch awkwardly and Bill's face was in shadow.

Then Dad cleared his throat importantly. 'Right, Small Fries! Gather round and I'll tell you exactly what is going on.'

Chapter 4
DAD'S SECRET

We all peered into the box. It was difficult to see much by torchlight. It was even more difficult to know what to say to Dad. I mean, the box didn't seem very special. In fact, it seemed full of perfectly ordinary packets of fish food called 'Fish Crisps'. But Dad was gazing at them as if they were the crown jewels.

'Er, Dad,' I said eventually, 'what *exactly* are we supposed to be looking *at*?'

'These,' said Dad, picking up a handful of crisp packets and raising them up into the air, 'are the Holy Grail of fish food.'

'*The Holy … what?*' screeched Stacey, trying to make herself heard above the noise of the radio.

But Dad stood like a man transfixed. 'The Holy Grail of fish food!' he said again. 'Look at these packets. Together they contain the finest ingredients, guaranteed to make fish fitter, healthier, bigger and better than ever before. Why, with these fish crisps we will be able to slake the hunger of any fish from minnows to whales, live they in the smallest fish tank or the biggest sea. With my new patent fish food, we will restock the oceans; replenish the lakes; re—'

By a strange coincidence, this rousing speech was accompanied by some loud sweeping orchestral music on the radio. It was all too much.

'Stop! Stop, Dad!' I begged, looking at his glowing cheeks and shining eyes. 'I'm sure they're really, really good. Truly I am. But why all this *fuss?*' I waved my hand around the room, pointing at the drawn curtains, the running taps and the loudly blaring radio.

Dad's eyes widened and he turned bright red. 'Because of *them!*' he muttered darkly.

'W-w-what do you mean, *"Them"*?' asked Mum, nervously. Dad leant forward so that we had to bend towards him to hear. And when we did, I must say I didn't believe him.

'Fish farmers!' whispered Dad, triumphantly.

'*Fish farmers?*' repeated Mum, disbelievingly. '*Fish farmers?* Surely *fish farmers* can't do us any harm?'

'Huh!' said Dad, rocking backwards importantly on his heels. 'That's what you might think, but how do *you* know? Those rascals would go to any lengths to get their hands on my fish food. There they are, busily farming their fish all over the world because the seas are running out of them. Then along I come with my packets of Super-Strong Fish Crisps. One or two rounds of the stuff in the sea and – poof! Hey presto! Bang goes their business.

And up go Finn's Fine Fish Foods' profits! The seas are full of fish; the fishing boats are full of fish; the shops are full of fish. Everyone is happy ... or everyone,' he lowered his voice again to a fierce whisper, 'except the fish farmers and our fiercest fish food competitors.' There was a dramatic pause. 'Ah, well ...' he added, cheering up and putting the crisps back into the box, 'I suppose it's technological breakthroughs like this that makes my job so worthwhile.'

He clicked off the torch and went to open the curtains, turn off the taps and switch off the music. I stared at him. I didn't get it. I mean, why bother? If the fish stocks in the seas are really that low, why don't we just stop eating fish? I certainly wouldn't object. I can't bear the stuff. But it didn't seem quite the right time to mention this. And anyway, Stacey had a question.

'But Dad, how are you going to make any money if you simply tip your fish food into the sea?'

'Ah, well, we're not – or at least not for a long time,' said Dad, a little confusingly. 'You see, we at Finn's Fine Fish Foods are developing two sorts of fish crisp: one that will be sold to the public for use at home, as well as to large zoos and aquariums; and a second type,' he paused and tapped the box, 'like this, which is being developed with government aid to help restock the seas. I call them the Super-Strong Fish Crisps for Scarce Sea Fish. This kind of fish crisp will be much, much stronger than the others. That's why this box here needs to be kept hidden somewhere safe, somewhere that fish farmers and their sort will never think to look.' He stopped talking and suddenly turned towards me. 'Somewhere like Ned's cupboard.'

'Ned's cupboard?' whispered Mum. 'But it stinks, and you can't get anywhere near it. His clothes are all over the floor in front of it!' Her voice was faint. Like me, she was probably reeling from the thought of a pack of angry fish farmers wearing yellow wellies and wielding fish hooks, rampaging through my dirty underwear.

'Exactly!' said Dad triumphantly. 'No one in their right mind would ever think of hiding such a valuable piece of research material there. Yes, this aquatic gold dust will be safe as houses in Ned's cupboard.'

Which is absolutely and exactly what it was not.

Chapter 5
CHANGING ROOMS

Have you ever had one of those dreams where everything goes wrong? I haven't, but I've heard of them, and if they are anything like what happened that afternoon I don't ever want to risk sleeping again.

As soon as Dad closed the box we all trooped upstairs to put it into my cupboard. In my room. (Well, obviously it was my room because that's where I sleep – or slept. Things move fast in my family.)

And that's when the Finn Family Upheaval began.

First of all, Bill was furious – even more furious and stroppy than he had been that morning. As soon as I opened the door, everybody saw what Mum calls The Mess and I just call General Living. (You know the sort of thing: clothes on the floor, shoes on the chairs, comics stuffed into the bin … nothing out of the ordinary.) But Bill immediately spotted The Books. And his Game Boy. On the bed. Where I'd been studying whilst pretending to be ill. He went ape. Mental. Ballistic. On a chart of one to ten he was at about nine trillion zillion. You see, it's one thing to be fobbed off by your older brother because he is – or at least claims to be – ill. It's quite another because he is swotting. That stinks. That sucks. As far as Bill was concerned I was a nerd and a geek and he was going to do three things. He would:

1. **Never speak to me again for the rest of his entire life, and he means that with nobs on so there.**

2. Ask for his Super-Zerio Inter-Galactic Game Boy game back, instantly, and if it's broken demand that it's replaced, with interest, out of my pocket money.
3. Ask Mum if he can have my room, because if all I'm going to do in it is lie in bed and read books then I might as well take a camp bed down to the local library and set up home there.

But Mum wasn't listening. She was worrying. Worrying that a load of yellow-wellied burglars would come into my room in the dead of night, and trip over my dirty socks in order to steal Dad's box. Worrying that I might get hurt. Worrying that I was sleeping alone.

'But Ned, Dan, this is *terrible*,' she said, clutching at my sleeve and surveying the scene.

Well, I must admit, it was bad.

'Really, really *awful*.'

I blinked and looked again. Well, I suppose it was a bit off to have stuffed Action Man head down in a glass of dirty water, but I didn't think it was actually putting the family at risk

And then Dad, trying to help, made it all a hundred times worse.

'Oh, no, Petal! This room's perfect! Don't worry!' he said, patting her comfortingly on the shoulder. He lifted the box and tried, unsuccessfully, to pick his way across the dross lying on the floor to the door of the cupboard. Something went crunch under his foot. It was Bill's Super-Zerio Inter-Galactic game for his Game Boy. I was dead. Utterly, totally caput.

Dad, of course, was as oblivious as ever. 'There's no problem,' he repeated reassuringly. 'All Ned needs to do is keep everything just the way it is. D'you hear that, Ned? No – and I mean absolutely *no* – tidying up!' And then he added the punch line, the one that will live in our household for the rest of time. 'But then, Ned's such a sensible boy, I know he can be relied upon!'

'*Sensible?*' Stacey's banshee wail could be heard halfway down the street. 'How can you even think that? Ned's nothing but a loser, a saddo … a … a total zero! *I'm* the reliable one! *I'm* the one who's always having to fix things for them at school!' (What has Stacey ever fixed apart from her hair?)

Because Mum seemed to be in a trance, it was left to Dad to calm Stacey down. 'Now hold on –' he stuttered. But he was too late. Stacey was in a state: a Martyr with a Mission – off to orbit Planet Stacey in a stellar-sized strop. We had no choice but to pin our ears back and hope that it wouldn't last any longer than usual.

But unfortunately for us, it did.

On and on she went. On and on and on. And on.

And, as ever, her strop followed the same well-worn pattern.

Strop One: *It's so unfair.*

'It's so unfair!' she shouted, waving her hands about at my crud-infested room. 'Just because I'm the only girl in this house –' (Mum, being over 30, clearly doesn't count) '– I get it in the neck. I mean – what *is* everyone complaining about? At least the stuff on my floor isn't a health hazard. My room is far, far tidier than this … this … *pigpen!*' (I reject this slur! I mean, let's face it; if my room is a tip, hers is a municipal dump!)

She broke off, struck by a sudden thought. Casting aside her handkerchief (well, actually, it was one of my vests, but I think we'll ignore that point), she looked up with a nasty glint in her eye that I know only too well. Strop Two was about to begin.

Strop Two: *How come he has more than me?*

'Hang on a moment,' she cried accusingly, assessing the room as though for the first time. 'How come Ned's got the biggest room anyway? He always has more than me! By rights, this should be my room! *I'm* the eldest! It's me who is the First Born Finn! I deserve respect! *I'm* the biggest child – so *I* should have the biggest room. *And by the way, Ned,*' she hissed, stabbing her finger in the air at me, 'before you say *anything*, when I say **big** – *I DON'T MEAN FAT!*'

Dad, eager to pour oil on troubled waters, tried to interrupt a second time. But he might as well not have bothered. Stamping her foot and behaving just like a heroine from a tacky TV soap, Stacey prepared to let rip on her two all-time favourite themes:

Strop Three: *1) Why do the boys always get more than me?*
2) Why do you love them more than me?

'I know why Ned's got this room! It's because he's a *boy*, isn't it? They always get what they want!' (NOT true! Don't forget the non-existent PlayStation!) 'I never get anything!' (Er, except for a lifetime's supply of super-strength, hard-as-nails hairspray.) 'It's so unfaaiiiir! You've always preferred the boys to me!' (Actually, if anything, I think Dad prefers fish on the basis that they Do Not Answer Back!)

And with this she took a deep breath and tossed her red mane of hair defiantly over her shoulder – a sure sign that we were about to start the Grand Slam (otherwise known as the Final Finn Flounce).

'Well, as far as I'm concerned, I've had it!' she screamed. 'Ned might be a swotty little goody two-shoes, but what about me? I mean, hello! Excuse me, but this is the twenty-first century! Hasn't anyone in this family heard about Women's Rights?' Then, before any of us had time to reply, she continued, 'No! Of course not! But that's oh-so typical of the way this family operates! I mean, does anyone ever consider me? No. Do they ever wonder about my needs? No. Do they listen? Can I ever get a word in edgeways?' (???!!!) 'Of course not! No one understands me! No one loves me. Everyone hates me! I'm all a-a-lone ... I can't take any mo-o-o-re ...!' she sobbed. But just as she was about to flounce out of the door (slamming it so hard that the windows rattled and the handle fell off), Mum came out of her trance and took the wind right out of her sails.

'Well, yes,' she said, briskly. 'Stacey's right!'

Stacey blinked, stopping in mid-flow. No one said anything – mainly because we were spreadeagled on the floor in shock.

Mum, ignoring the silence, continued on briskly 'Stacey can have this room … Ned can move into the top bunk bed in Bill's room.' Bill stamped his foot in fury, but realised from the look on Mum's face that she was not in the mood for discussion. 'And then we can turn Stacey's old room into a study for Ned – look at the books all over the bed; he's obviously trying to study, bless him. I know it's going to be tough on Bill, but we'll try and make it up to him somehow …' Then, noticing that we were still unconvinced, she started to falter. 'Well, maybe you'll enjoy sharing after all this time,' she added lamely. 'After all, hah hah,' she tittered nervously, catching sight of Bill's tight-lipped jaw, 'it might be nice for you to spend a bit of quality time together …'

She looked beseechingly at Bill, but he was having none of it. He just wanted time to plunge me up to my neck in a vat of boiling oil. The truth was etched all over his face. Not only did he *not* get my old room, he didn't get Stacey's either – and that was twice as big as his. Instead, all he had ended up with was me, my dirty underwear and a load of unwanted junk. There was no escaping the facts. I had moved in one fell swoop from being the Most Disliked Person in the Room to being Mr Evil, Public Enemy Number One.

But just as all seemed up with me, Dad fired off a second bombshell. For once in his life, he disagreed with Mum.

'No, Plankton,' he said in a firm voice, ignoring Stacey's outraged squeal. 'This is not going to work.'

Well, of course it wasn't. I could have told him that. Nothing ever works in this house.

'Stacey cannot live with Ned's cupboard in her room,' Dad continued.

'Why not?' I protested. Until five minutes ago, I had spent my entire life in the company of that cupboard.

'Stacey is a Girl,' said Dad, somewhat stating the obvious. 'Say what she might about Female Rights, she might be in danger here on her own.'

'Oh, Dad, you're so thoughtful,' said Stacey, reaching up and kissing him on the cheek. 'I'd be *so* worried if I thought those horrid fish farmers were going to sneak into the room and scare me half to death.' To be honest, I couldn't agree. One snarl from her and I think they'd be off back to their lochs and lakes in an instant. They wouldn't stand a chance against her cutting comments and bright blue talons.

But Stacey hadn't finished. Aware that she had an audience, she snuggled up to Dad. 'And I would,' she added, looking round the room, 'find it difficult to keep the room as messy as this, however hard I tried. You see, I'm naturally an organised person.' And here she looked daggers at me. Ouch, does my sister know how to twist that knife. Do you think it's something that girls learn at nursery school?

That clinched it. Stacey was given the big room – *my* bedroom; and the cupboard – *my* cupboard – was moved to Bill's – now *our* – bedroom.

Of course it didn't fit. So we had to change the beds round so that they were crammed against one wall directly facing the cupboard. This meant it was quite awkward to get in and out of the bunks. By now Bill was definitely not talking to anyone – which is always a bad sign. Anyhow, with a lot of huffing and puffing we managed to squeeze the cupboard in, open the door just far enough and wedge the box of fish crisps inside. But it wasn't something I would want to do more than once.

No, I reckoned that Dad, this time, was right. Any burglar aiming to do a dirty dart into our room to steal the box, would find he had his work cut out.

We were safe.

We could relax.

We could, perhaps, even have lunch. I was starving. Even boiled cod and seaweed sludge sounded delicious by now.

But lunch was off the menu. Mum had a mission: to make the rest of the house presentable enough to be fingered by the fussiest fish farmer. This left Dad to prepare lunch (never a clever move) and Stacey and I to argue over who should be the first to pick the pink chewing gum off the bed post.

So it wasn't until later that we realised that Bill was missing.

Chapter 6 BILL GOES MISSING

Things weren't going well.

A whole hour had passed since we'd moved rooms and we were still in total chaos. Dad's burnt lunch had set off the fire alarm and it was now bleeping fit to burst, making the dog bark non-stop. Mum kept yelling down the stairs for one of us to shut the kitchen door and wave a tea towel at the alarm, but if Dad heard, he certainly hadn't understood. The high-pitched din was now threatening to out-squeal even Stacey's squawks.

As for the rest of the mess ... well, I was faintly embarrassed, now that I came to look at it – a motley assortment of clothes, trainers, books, half-eaten sweets, scrunched up-crisp packets and abandoned toys. I took some comfort from Stacey's ex-bedroom floor which was littered with make-up and magazines. Bill's was scattered with catapults (broken), pebbles, bits of wood, the jawbone he'd found on the heath, a hammer Dad had lost almost a year ago and some unfinished Lego models. When I tried to suggest to Mum that mine wasn't bad in comparison, she silently pointed to Glam Gran's missing pension book (reported stolen), the missing keys to the car we sold three years ago, a Tupperware box containing a festering cheese sandwich that she had made for my school trip last month, and worst of all, the first jumper she ever knitted me in hideous, rainbow-coloured stripes. My claim that the dog must have eaten it had led to our poor mutt being banished to her kennel for a week.

Mum was clearly so hurt and angry that she could hardly speak. She simply turned round and hissed for me to go *at once* and tell my brother to come back *this minute* to help. I took one look at her face and beat a hasty retreat. But I couldn't resist drawing her attention to Stacey's newly created sign for 'her' bedroom door.

The new Queen of Clean had written:

Dear Fish Farmers
Dad's Super-Strong
Fish Crisps for
Scarce Sea Fish
ARE NEXT DOOR
(in Ned's cupboard)
← Love
Stacey x

The arrow pointed directly towards Bill's room.

Stacey refused to take it down. Soon she and Mum were going at each other hammer and tongs. She also refused to have anything to do with my mess. 'I'm not touching one single smelly sock!' she yelled. 'They're so rank. I mean, what does Ned *do* with his stuff? Sniff this ...' and, to prove her point, she grabbed one of my old trainers and tried to shove it up Mum's nose.

Luckily Stacey's new mobile phone started to bleep, saving me from any more abuse. It was her best friend, Irritating Izzy. The phone glued to her left ear, Stacey forgot all about tidying up our room

– or rather rooms – and started moaning on about Mum and Dad and me and Bill, my books, my pathetic attempts at swotting, my need for a brain as well as a study, the meanness of life/family/friends ... oh yes, and the colour of their friend Tracey's new hair extensions and which film star looked best in the recent Oscar parade. That mobile phone. One beep and she was back on Planet Stacey in her own parallel universe.

Mum finally flipped. Yanking the phone out of Stacey's hand, she pushed her in the direction of a teetering pile of old magazines and bellowed (well, it was the only tone of voice Mum had left at that point) for Bill. But no one came. Bill had vanished.

Normally, Bill going AWOL* would put everyone on Red Alert as it could mean only one of two things:

1. Bill was busy getting into Trouble.
2. Bill had got into Trouble and now Trouble was busy waiting to get its own back on him.

*Absent Without Leave

But things were not normal – not normal at all.

I looked everywhere I could think of in the house without success, so I decided to search the garden. I tried the bushes … The tree house … The garden shed … but I couldn't find him anywhere. Bill had vanished.

I love our garden. It is one of the best things about our house. It's huge and overgrown and a great place to play. When Glam Gran lived here the garden was full of flowers and neatly cut lawns. But now that she has given the house to us and spends her time shopping and sightseeing abroad, the whole place has been left to grow wild. Everywhere, that is, except for the ornamental pond.

The pond, which is at the bottom of the garden and out of sight of the house, is Dad's pride and joy. It has a large stone fountain and is completely weed-free. It's here that Dad keeps all his prize fish, including Goldie-the-Goldfish – he knows them all by name. It's one of Dad's favourite places. Bill likes it too, which is why I was convinced he might be here.

I crept cautiously towards the pond, hoping to surprise my brother. I don't really like water – which perhaps explains why I don't really like fish. Water makes me nervous, especially when it's anywhere near Bill. It gives him a chance to get up to – or get into – trouble. But there was no one there. Instead, floating on the surface of the pool, were two empty packets of Dad's new patent fish crisps.

My heart started to thump. I felt an icy chill run up and down my spine. How could the packets have got there? Dad was in the kitchen, making (or *trying* to make lunch). Mum and Stacey were locked in the mother of all Bedroom Battles. So who else could possibly have found these packets of fish crisps? No one – unless … I froze, gripped by a terrible thought. Unless, perhaps, they had already been stolen by a fish farmer! And if some fish farmers had managed to get their hands on Dad's fish food, could they also have managed to get their hands on Bill, too? I picked up a large stout stick and tried to be brave. I felt a bit of an idiot, but how did I know who was lurking in the trees around me?

There was a sudden movement in the water, followed by splashing and gurgling noises. My heart leapt. 'Bill!' I shouted, edging towards the pond. I peered into the water, still clutching my stick.

All I could see was Goldie the outsize goldfish, slowly swimming backwards and forwards.

Then something caught my eye. Just behind Goldie there was a large, ugly fish that I had never seen before: a huge cod, with what looked like a single golden curl coming out of the top of its head. I swear it looked familiar. Too surprised to be frightened I crouched down on to my hands and knees to take a closer look.

'B-Bill?' I faltered, uncertainly.

THWACK! No sooner had I muttered his name, than the ugly cod jumped out of the water and smacked me hard across the forehead, leaving a nasty smelly smear of fish scales all over my fringe.

'OWWW!' I yelled at the top of my voice, falling backwards. 'You stupid, stupid fish, what on earth did you do that for? That hurt!' I glared at the pool, but the fish had disappeared.

'Wretched fish!' I shouted out to no one in particular. 'If there are any fish farmers here, they are welcome to any packets of Dad's food they can find!' And so saying I stomped back into the house in an absolute grump. Bill or no Bill, I wanted my lunch and at that point I did not want to go near any kind of pond or hear the word 'fish' ever again.

Chapter 7

THE MIS-TAKE

When I got back to the house, Dad had set the toaster on fire for the second time, and by the time we had doused the flames everyone had forgotten about Bill. It was probably something to do with the hunger pangs. I had even (temporarily) forgotten about the two mysteriously empty packets of Dad's fish food floating on the pond – and being slapped in the face by a cod. All I could think about was lunch – or the lack of it. Dad had given up; Stacey was in a huff and, with the air of a martyr, said she couldn't possibly make lunch because she was too busy tidying up her room *alone*; and Mum was knitting.

This is always a bad sign. Mum's a worrier by nature and when she's worried, she knits. She collects odd bits of left-over organically dyed wool which she turns into strange jumpers and socks that she expects us to wear. Looking at her white face and trembling hands, I reckoned we were in for a flock of virulent orange tank tops.

I sighed. This was an emergency. I picked up the phone. I speed-dialled straight through to the local pizza delivery shop and within ten minutes we were sitting down to a feast of tomato and mozzarella double-thick pizzas, garlic bread and dough balls. All except Mum who said that she'd have an organic bean salad once she'd completed a particularly intricate part of her knitting pattern. As soon as the pizza boxes were opened, Bill appeared. Honestly, my brother can smell a chocolate bar being unwrapped at fifty paces.

Pizza is his second favourite food. It's amazing.

What was also amazing was that:

1. Bill was in a really good mood.
2. He was ever so slightly damp and there was a long, straggly bit of green pond weed hanging over his left ear.

Mum looked at him suspiciously, put down her knitting, and felt his clothes.

'Bill, what have you been up to?' she asked worriedly.

Bill, whose mouth was already crammed full of dough balls, looked a bit shifty.

Mum picked up her knitting again and said, 'Well, I think you should go upstairs and get changed … You'll catch your death in that damp sweatshirt.'

'Now, now, Petal!' Dad said, eager as ever to help. 'I almost forgot. There's no need to worry! I've got just the thing!' He rummaged about in the white plastic carrier bag he had brought home that morning and pulled out a small, brightly coloured packet. 'Here you are, Bill,' he said, ripping it open and shaking out its contents. 'Our company's brand new T-shirt. You'll be the first to try it on!' He waved it about with a flourish. 'What do you think? Good, eh?'

Bill stared at the T-shirt in shock. 'But Dad, it's bright pink!' he protested in disgust.

'And it's covered in swirly green writing!' added Stacey, pointing to the words 'Finn's Fine Fish Foods' daubed across its back.

'And why does it have a picture of a killer whale saying, "Moo!" on the front?' I asked.

Dad looked at me pityingly and chuckled gently to himself.

'Moo? No, no, Ned. It says "Boo!" The killer whale is saying "Boo!" It's a joke.' He tapped his finger on the side of his nose. 'It's what we in the trade call a *marketing ploy*. It's there to catch the attention of the public!' Looking a bit sheepish, he coughed and said, 'You see, with all the excitement, I haven't had time to tell you, but we've won the contract at the zoo to feed their new killer whale – you know, the one they rescued from that Hollywood film set recently? Well, it arrives next week – along with their new Marine Life Manager – and I thought it would be a good idea to advertise the fact. After all, what's good enough for a magnificent beast like a killer whale is good enough for any old fishbowl.'

Dad was on a roll. He leant forward, keen to share his enthusiasm. 'It doesn't do to waste these opportunities for a bit of promotion. So I thought it would be great if you kids could go to the aquarium and hand out these T-shirts with some free samples of my fish food. Look,' he said, picking up the T-shirt, 'the zoo's given the old aquarium a state-of-the-art makeover – you can see it at the back of the pic …'

His voice trailed off as he studied the picture more closely. Then he shouted, 'Ruddy Geoff! I'll murder him! No wonder these were so cheap! All that dratted man can think about are his cows! Look at that mistake!' He stabbed his finger at the word 'Moo' on the T-shirt he was holding. 'He's printed the wrong word! I'm going to kill him!'

'Oh, Dan,' Mum wailed, her needles clacking together at double speed. 'Tell me you didn't use Geoff to print your T-shirts?'

Dad nodded, dumbly. The penny had finally dropped.

Geoff – or Grotty Geoff, as he is known locally – is Dad's best friend and the worst printer in town. He can't spell, he can hardly see and he's obsessed with cows in the same way that Dad is with fish. He sneaks pictures of them on to everything he prints. The whole town is littered with signposts and billboards decorated for no good reason with pictures of Friesian bulls and Jersey calves. Only Dad would have hired someone like Geoff to print a T-shirt. But then, Dad *is* a fashion zero. He hasn't got a clue when it comes to clothes. He's the only man I know who thinks 'smart casual' means wearing a kipper tie with a rugby shirt.

'Well, I'm sorry, Dad, but there's no way I'll be seen in one of those!' sneered Stacey, flicking her hair.

'No, no, of course not,' said Mum reassuringly,

starting off on another ball of wool. Goodness knew who she was making this jumper for, but I reckoned it would on their back by teatime. 'I'm sure we can do something to sort this all out. We'll just ask Geoff to print some more. We might even be able to change their colour a bit.' She looked at Dad. 'I know pink is really eye-catching, but it doesn't really go with Stacey's ginger hair, does it?'

Stacey ground her teeth. '*Auburn*, not ginger,' she muttered, tossing her carrot-red mane everywhere.

Mum ignored her and turned back to Dad. 'Now, tell me, Dan. How many T-shirts did you say you had printed?'

Dad looked in the air and then down at his toes. 'Twenty,' he said casually. 'Yup, about twenty would be about right.'

'Well, then,' said Mum, smiling, 'there's nothing to worry about, is there? We'll just get another twenty printed.'

'No,' said Dad, pushing his toe into the kitchen rug and refusing to meet Mum's eye. 'I don't think you quite understand. I meant twenty – er *thousand*. I've got twenty thousand T-shirts printed with the words "Just say Moo!" sitting in the garage. Do you think I might have over-ordered?'

Chapter 8
JOE THE BULLY

The rest of the week passed in a bit of a haze. Only Bill seemed happy. In fact, he seemed remarkably cheerful. He kept disappearing for hours on end and coming back with a big grin on his face, smelling faintly of rotten fish. I was dead suspicious. Try as I might, I could not figure out what he was up to or where he went. He'd vanish as if into thin air. No one else noticed. But then, we were all rather busy trying to work out what to do with the lorry load of misprinted T-shirts that Dad had stacked in the garage.

Mum and Dad couldn't bear the thought of

upsetting Geoff by asking him to print the T-shirts a second time, especially when Dad told Mum Geoff had done them on the cheap as a bit of a favour. He had printed them as part of a special T-shirt deal he was doing for the annual Cattlebury Cattle Show. What made it even worse was that he simply couldn't see what was wrong with them. In fact, Geoff was convinced that everyone at the cattle show or the zoo would buy one.

We tried to persuade Mum and Dad to burn them or at least take them to the dump, but Mum wouldn't hear of it. There were too many of them and, anyway, she hates waste. Her view was that if Dad was in a mess it was up to us to do our best to help him sort it out. She would brook no argument. We were to go to the zoo that weekend and:

1. **Try to get rid of (sorry, 'hand out') as many of Dad's crummy T-shirts and packets of Fish Crisps as we could.**

And (much worse):

2. **I had to look after Bill.**

I mean honestly, why me? Why
not Stacey? But there was
nothing I could do. Bill smiled his
most angelic smile and promised
to be good. He said he couldn't
wait to go to the zoo and that
he was really looking forward to
seeing the new aquarium. He even
insisted on packing the rucksack for
Mum. Looking back, I should have
realised that he was up to something. By the time I
did, it was far, far too late.

Saturday morning proved to be every bit as bad as
we feared.

Dad made us get up really early so as not to miss
a single punter at the zoo. We didn't mind very
much. The earlier we got there, the sooner we
could get away. But we reckoned without Dad.

Although he was too shy (or embarrassed) to go
out and sell the T-shirts himself, he couldn't help
interfering. He kept spying on us from behind
bushes and whispering instructions. If anyone
looked vaguely interested, he would hiss loudly at
us and wave his arms about like a madman. But as
soon as they read the slogan on the T-shirts, they'd

laugh and walk away. No one was remotely interested in taking a sample of the fish food.

In the end, even Dad gave up. Sighing deeply, he left for home. He looked so dejected and miserable that it was difficult not to feel sorry for him. We decided to stay on and hope that things improved. Otherwise, what was Dad going to do with all his worthless stock?

We were just trying to think round the problem, when something happened that turned a bad situation even worse. Joe Blagg, the school bully, arrived.

My heart sank. Joe is the kind of boy who's nobody's friend and everyone's enemy. He's a greedy, idle layabout with sharp, beady eyes that peak out from behind a thick fringe of unwashed hair. Even the teachers are frightened of him as his mother has a habit of biffing them with her handbag if they ever dare to complain about his behaviour. I had spent all year avoiding Joe's attention, mainly by keeping out of his way. But as soon as I saw that glint in his eye that morning I knew my time was up.

'Well, well, well,' he drawled thickly through a mouthful of food. He sauntered up to us. 'If it isn't the three thick Finns.' He laughed at his joke. 'Let's see, what does your T-shirt say?' He leant forward and stared at my chest. 'Oh, yes, I see: "Just say Moo!" Ha! Ha! That's got to be a misprint. But then you've probably been to Grotty Geoff the printer. It's all your kind can afford! *"Just say Moo!"* Well, Ginger,' he sneered, turning to Stacey and smirking, 'I suppose it's slightly better to turn into a cow than a carrot top – but you can tell your dad from me that I think his T-shirts are a load of old bull!'

He stopped short and suddenly had an idea. You could tell when Joe Blagg had an idea because it lit up his face, rather like a single light bulb in a blackened room.

'A load of old bull – I made a joke! Fish – moo – cow – bull! Geddit?!' He collapsed in a fit of laughter.

I gritted my teeth and struggled not to rise. In the end, it was Bill who cracked first. Dad might be eccentric, but no one criticises him in front of us and gets away with it. Unable to restrain himself, Bill ran forward and tried to kick Joe in the shins.

I joined him from behind. Stacey, angry at being called 'Ginger' and 'Carrot Top' when everyone knows she is, in reality, a strawberry blonde, yelled encouragement. Joe dodged us neatly and then, sticking two fat fingers in his mouth, gave a piercing whistle. Instantly, as though out of fresh air, his two henchmen, Thrasher and Crasher, appeared. We were in big trouble. Between them, those three had the strength of a hammerhead shark. We ducked and ran.

Joe, Thrasher and Crasher lumbered after us all over the zoo: up by the chimpanzees, down by the giraffes and along past the snake house. Finally, we ended up at the aquarium. There was simply nowhere else to go – and no way out except the way we had come. The aquarium itself was a large, round, steep-sided tank surrounded by a semicircle of concrete steps and uncomfortable plastic seats. There was a battered digger and a pile of stones to one side of the pool where someone was obviously trying to create a new water feature. On the other, there was a long articulated lorry with a huge container on the back.

Panting and out of breath, we crouched behind the seats and waited for Joe and his cohorts to come round the corner. But they never arrived. When it was clear that they'd given up the chase — presumably distracted by the hot dog stand next to the penguin enclosure — I sat up and tried to work out what to do. I was pretty sure that Joe, Thrasher and Crasher would wait for us at the exit to the zoo. Our best chance was to sit it out in the aquarium and hope that, in time, the bullies would give up and go home. Even Bill, who can't bear waiting for anything, thought it was the best plan.

Half an hour passed.

Then another.

Bill began to run out of patience. 'I'm hungry,' he complained. 'Very, *very* hungry.'

In an effort to distract him, I pointed out a badly printed sign nearby. It said:

COMING SOON!
KYLIE THE KILLER WHALE
SHE IS 10 METRES LONG, HAS 48
TEETH AND WEIGHS 4,000 KILOS

In the bottom left-hand corner you could just see a tiny picture of an Aberdeen Angus bull wearing a red rosette. I sighed. Grotty Geoff had been at it again.

Stacey was unimpressed.

'*Kylie,*' she cried, disgustedly, '*Kylie!* What kind of name is that for a killer whale?'

Bill nodded. 'I agree,' he said decisively, peering into the empty water. 'Kylie will be bored and hungry – just like me.' He turned round and fixed me with a set of beseeching eyes, like a puppy that hasn't been fed for a week. 'Ne-e-e-e-e-d,' he wheedled, 'are you sure you don't have any food left? I'm starving.'

I groaned. Since we had arrived at the zoo, Bill had demolished two packets of crisps, a chocolate bar and some mouldy toffees that had been stuck to the inside of my trouser pocket. Anything he hadn't eaten had been devoured by my sister, Miss Sweetie-holic herself. I scrabbled around in the backpack to check there was nothing I'd missed.

'Nope! Sorry! You're out of luck,' I said finally. 'All I've got left are Dad's packets of fish crisps.'

Bill didn't mind. He wasn't fussy. Before I had time to think, Bill seized his chance, grabbing a couple of packets and ripping them open.

'You can't eat that stuff!' I protested. 'You don't

66

know what's in it.'

'Too late,' mumbled Bill, his eyes shining above his bulging cheeks.

I stared at him, unable to believe how stupid he'd been. But before I could come up with a suitably crushing comment, I was distracted by a noise from behind. A tall woman was wobbling her way up the slope on a pair of impossibly high-heeled shoes, accompanied by several officials. She was carrying a megaphone and was obviously not in a good mood. I was just trying to puzzle out what was going on when Bill touched me on the arm.

'Uh, oh, Ned,' he said quickly, 'I think I feel a little fishy.'

'What do you mean?' I asked him. But before Bill could answer. There was a sudden flash, bang and whizz and somehow, some way, my six-year-old brother dived into the aquarium. Bill had disappeared and there, in the water, was a grubby grey cod with an unmistakable grin on its face and a single golden curl coming out of the top of its head.

Chapter 9
BILL IN TROUBLE!

I couldn't believe what had just happened.

One moment my brother was standing next to me, whining about being hungry. The next, there was a cod swimming happily about in the tank grinning just like Bill – and looking *remarkably* like the one that had jumped out of our fish-pond and slapped me on my fringe. Stacey and I rushed to the side of the pool and peered in, our mouths opening and closing in shock.

'Look at me!' cried the bizarre-looking cod (apparently fish that have once been boys can talk). 'Aren't I clever?' He did a backflip. If ever a cod could look smug, this one did.

Clever? I simply couldn't believe my eyes. 'Bill,

Bill! What's happened to you?' I shouted. 'What on earth have you done?'

'He's turned into a f-iiii-sh!' cried Stacey. Then she burst into tears. 'Do something!' she ordered me. 'Change him back!'

I rolled my eyes. I don't mean to be unhelpful or anything, but changing a younger brother back from being a cod into a boy is not part of my day-to-day routine. What exactly did she expect me to do?

Bill, of course, didn't seem in the least bit concerned. 'Oh, don't worry! Watch this,' he called cheerfully, doing a double somersault out of the water. 'This is fantastic. You have to come in, Stacey, the water's great! All you need to do is shovel a couple of handfuls of Dad's fish crisps into your mouth!'

Stacey cheered up immediately. 'OK,' she said, 'I will. How many packets do you think I'll need?' And she ran back to rummage in the rucksack.

I acted fast. 'Look,' I snapped, grabbing it from her. 'There is NO way I'm going to allow you to become a fish too. One cod in the family is quite enough, thank you.'

'It's not fair,' wailed Stacey, as per usual. 'Why do you and Bill always have more fun than I do?'

'*Fun ...! Fun?*' I cried, in disbelief. This wasn't Fun; this was classic Bill – Trouble with a capital T. 'This is a disaster! How on earth are we going to explain this to Mum? I can just see us going home and saying: "Mum, you know you asked us to take Bill to the zoo and make sure he didn't get into any trouble? Well, we had a great time, except that Bill accidentally turned into a fish – we left him swimming around in a large tank that is about to become home to a not-so-friendly killer whale."'

I stared at Bill in horror. What would happen if we couldn't change him back? Or if Joe and his buddies came round the corner and found out what was going on? I tried to keep calm. At the very least, I had to get Bill out of the tank. I just needed to work out how.

My first instinct was to ask for help. The seats around the aquarium were beginning to fill up – but how could I explain what had happened? Everyone would think we were mad! No, I had to face facts. Bill was in Trouble – and it was up to me to sort it out.

Looking round, I saw a bucket at the bottom of the steps. 'Right, Bill,' I said, trying to sound reassuring. 'Leave it to me! I'll get you out of there just as soon as I can! Whatever you do, keep calm!'

'Take your time, bro!,' said Bill, concentrating more on his triple somersault than on what I was saying.

I picked up the
bucket and, ignoring my fear of
water, tried to reach over the side
of the pool to dangle it into
the tank. But I wasn't quite tall
enough to reach over. Nor was
Stacey.

'Stacey!' I yelled, thinking fast. 'Take
this bucket and guard it with your life. I'm going to
find a ladder. Now, whatever you do, *don't leave Bill
alone.*'

Stacey, who had stopped crying, clutched the bucket and tried to look brave. And then, just as I thought that matters couldn't get any worse, they did. There was a loud crackling noise overhead and the tannoy system buzzed into action.

'Ahem! Ladies and gentlemen,' boomed a loud high-pitched female voice. 'We here at the zoo are proud to present for the very first time and two days earlier than advertised, the arrival – all the way from Hollywood in the US of A of that terrifying and death-defying monster – Kylie the killer whale!'

And with those words, the underwater gates of the aquarium slid open and four thousand kilos of black and white killer whale entered the tank.

Chapter 10

RESCUE!

Let's recap:

1. Bill, my brother, has turned into a cod and is swimming around in a large aquarium.
2. He has just been joined there by Kylie, a highly-toned killer whale. Kylie looks hungry. My brother is the only food on offer.
3. The sole way I can save Bill-the-fish is to turn him back into Bill-the-boy. Unfortunately, I don't have a clue how to do this.

4. Conclusion: Kylie is going to think Bill is her fish and chips and I am going to . . .

PPPPPAAAAAAAAAANNNNNNIIIIIC!!!

'Quick, pass me the bucket!' I yelled at Stacey. Grabbing her shoulders with both hands, I hauled myself up on to her back and leant over the rails. By standing on Stacey's shoulders, I could just get the bucket into the water. Stacey, protesting loudly, staggered around trying to balance my weight.

'Stop squishing my eyes!' she moaned. But I didn't care. Our brother could be a pain in the neck, but I didn't want him to end up as Kylie's fish supper.

'Keep swimming!' I yelled at Bill.

'I am!' he shouted back. And he was. In fact, I have never seen a fish swim so fast. He was diving, pirouetting, jumping and flipping. But it was no good. Kylie, who obviously relished the sport, had noticed him and was closing in fast. I could sense it would not be long before Bill ran out of energy.

'Try and distract her,' I shouted, as I failed once again to catch Bill in the bucket as he shot past.

'How?' my brother asked breathlessly as he

narrowly dodged one of Kylie's fins.

'I don't know,' I snapped back, irritated. 'Tell her some jokes, ask her about herself. If you can look like a fish, maybe you can speak fish too!' The gathering crowd was having a ball. They thought we were a warm-up act and were beginning to clap and cheer.

There was another crackling noise from above. The bossy lady's voice again began to address the crowd that was now rushing to take their seats.

'Welcome, welcome, everyone – boys and girls, mums and dads,' she said. There was a pause and then the sound of a fingernail tapping the microphone. 'Come on now, hurry up,' she continued, a little tetchily. 'There's room for everyone. Well, there would be, if you were slim and beautiful like me – but then,' there was a sigh, 'I suppose it would be impossible to be so perfect ... I have just been to HOLLYWOOD, you know, to collect this stinking – I mean, er, this *beautiful* whale ...' She coughed and regained her composure, continuing in honeyed tones, 'So, *please* take your time – take all the time you need to get to your seats – BUT JUST DON'T BE ALL DAY ABOUT IT!' she snapped.

There was another pause as the speaker struggled to control her temper again.

'Now, today is the big day – AND NO, IT'S *NOT* MY FAULT THAT IT'S EARLY – HONESTLY, TRYING TO GET ANYTHING DONE TO A TIMETABLE IN THIS TINPOT COUNTRY IS IMPOSS—' She broke off as her voice became increasingly shrill.

'Of course, I mean that due to unforeseen circumstances, we are *thrilled* to announce, two days earlier than we thought possible, the arrival of Kylie, the killer whale, our great star of the Hollywood screen – BUT NOT AS BIG A STAR

AS ME, DONNA MEZZWEME, THE MAGNIFICENT MANAGER, THE ZEALOUS ZOO KEEPER, THE … THE … THE ACNE OF AQUARIAS!'

There was a puzzled silence and a reluctant ripple of applause. Stacey and I weren't the only ones around that aquarium staring at each other in amazement. Was she really comparing herself to a face full of zits? But before we could say anything, the loudspeaker system burst once more into life.

'Goodness me!' said the voice excitedly. 'Kylie seems very lively. Would you look at that whale GO? You'd think, after a transatlantic flight she'd be a little jet-lagged, like me …'

There followed a hastily smothered yawn and an awkward cough. It was then that Donna Mezzweme noticed us, still desperately trying to catch Bill in the bucket.

'What are those children doing down there!' she snapped. 'I don't believe it! Are they trying to play with our killer whale?'

There was a gasp of disapproval from the crowd whilst everyone in the audience turned to look at Stacey and me.

Then the voice barked out, all friendliness

vanished: 'Stewards, stewards, GRAB THOSE KIDS! Get them out of there!'

The crowd turned against us and leant forward, pointing their fingers and craning their necks to see what would happen next. Somehow, I didn't think now was the quite the right time to explain that we weren't *playing* with Kylie, we were in a Finn-to-fin struggle for Bill's life. And it wasn't clear which Finn would win. Bill was jumping here, there and everywhere. I was sloshing about with a bucket, and Stacey was staggering up and down the edge of the pool trying to hold me upright. Suddenly some of the spectators realised what was going on.

They started to cheer and stand up to get a better look. The buzz of interest grew louder. But Stacey and I were only interested in getting Bill into our grimy bucket. We only had seconds left to save our brother from the jaws of death. As the stewards arrived, I saw Kylie's great tooth-filled jaw rise up from the water, ready for the kill. With one last effort, Bill dashed towards us and leapt in a great arc in the air. The crowd gasped. Everyone – including the stewards held their breath. There was an enormous splash and Bill landed safely in our pail. A huge cheer went up. We had done it! Bill was safe! Shaking with fright, Stacey and I collapsed on the ground in a heap, clutching the bucket between us.

'Don't worry,' panted Bill-the-cod, from the bucket. 'Kylie's not angry, she's just laughing. I took your advice and told her a joke.'

I stared down at him blankly.

'I asked her what you would you get if you crossed a duck-billed platypus with a plonker like my sister.' He waited for us to answer and when we didn't, he continued, 'A duck-nosed plonker-puss, of course!'

Bill, still in the bucket, roared with laughter.

Sometimes, I really think I could *kill* my brother.

Chapter 11 FAME

You might have thought that things would improve at that point, but after we had rescued Bill, they became even more difficult.

Bill, thankfully, had somehow remained in the bucket of water. Stacey, who had landed in a heap underneath me, was rolling around on the ground with my foot in her face (a mistake, I maintain). The crowd was clapping and cheering.

None of this impressed Donna Mezzweme. She came tottering towards us on her high-heeled shoes. Her dyed yellow hair was piled up on her head in a bun that wobbled as she walked. She was wearing the largest pair of dark sunglasses I had ever seen, even though it was a dull day. Her face was puce with anger.

'What on earth do you think you're doing?' she snapped, eyeing us suspiciously.

I sighed. It was not going to be easy to explain our way out of this mess.

'Sorry,' I muttered. 'We were just saving this, er, cod.'

'Saving a cod?' she repeated disbelievingly. She peered into the bucket, unable to lean down very far because her skirt was so tight. Bill smirked and did his best to look appealing. Donna Mezzweme was not impressed. 'Eeeeeeuch,' she sniffed, stepping backwards in disgust. 'I've never seen such an ugly fish.' She paused and jabbed a perfectly painted red talon at Bill. 'Is that *hair* sticking out of its head?'

Bill stuck his tongue out at her and, as she jumped back in alarm, she was distracted by a shout from the crowd.

'That boy's a hero!' someone cried. 'He saved that tiny fish from the killer whale. Let's give him a round of applause.' Everyone started to clap. And the next thing I knew, a reporter from the local newspaper had rushed up to take a picture of us all.

'Well, well,' tittered Donna insincerely, 'I suppose everything has turned out for the best.' Pushing her sunglasses to the top of her head, she patted her hair into place, tugged at her skirt and reapplied a thick layer of lipstick. Striking a pose, she pouted and smiled smugly at the camera. Then she hissed under her breath, 'Now, look, my name is Donna Mezzweme. I am the new Marine Life Manager. And *you* ...' she sneered as she read our T-shirts, '*you* must be Dan Finn's children. Well, I don't care how good his fish crisps are, you can tell your dad from me that HE'S LOST HIS CONTRACT and that I *never* want to see you or your cod near Kylie again.'

She needn't have worried. Stacey, Bill and I had had enough of whales to last three lifetimes. It had been a tiring day. Nodding goodbye to the reporter and with the cheers of the crowd ringing in my ears, I picked up my brother in the bucket and quietly sloped off home with Stacey. My head was buzzing with worries:

1. What was Dad going to say when he discovered he'd lost his contract to feed the killer whale?
2. How would Mum react when she read all about this in the local paper? And above all:

3. What were we going to do with Bill?

4. How long could we hide him in a bucket?
5. And how on earth were we going to turn him from a fish back into a boy?

HIDDEN DEPTHS

gorgeous

When we reached home, we had our first piece of luck in a week. The house was empty. Mum, thinking Dad was with us at the zoo, had gone out.

> *Gone to get my hair done*
> *Back at one*
> *Love Mum*
> *xxx*

'Quick!' I shouted to Stacey. 'Go and fill the bath!'

Stacey, for once, didn't argue. She charged up the stairs and turned on the cold tap full blast.

'Ouch!' went Bill, as we turned the bucket upside

down and dumped him into the water. 'Mind my nose!' He swam unenthusiastically up and down the bath a few times. 'It's not nearly so much fun as the aquarium,' he said, sulking. 'The water's too cold and it's far too shallow to dive –'

'Well, at least you're not sharing your bath with a killer whale,' I snapped back, exasperated.

'That's true,' replied Bill amiably. 'Although I have to say we got on pretty well, considering.' He paused and then said, 'I know. If I can't dive, I'll try something else.' And before I knew what was happening, he had flipped up on to his tail and was ricocheting back and forth the length of the bath, stirring up water. 'Hey, wheelies!' he cried happily.

'Oh, Bill, you are clever!' cried Stacey, clapping her hands. 'You've turned the bath into a jacuzzi!'

'A ja-cod-zi, more like!' laughed Bill. 'This is great!'

I groaned. Matters were quite bad enough without Bill making terrible fish jokes. He was beginning to sound just like Dad. And as for the bathroom, there was water everywhere. I bent down on the floor and tried to mop it up with one of Mum's pink fluffy towels.

'Now, look, Your Almighty Codliness,' I said, deciding that two can play Fish Puns, 'I'll put you back in that bucket if you don't stop codding around.' I wrung the towel out over the bath and eyed him suspiciously. 'Are you *quite* sure this is the first time you've ever turned into a fish?'

Bill ignored my question. 'Hey! This is the best fun I've had in ages. And don't worry, I'm sure I'll turn back into a boy at some point. I just need to wait for the effect of the food to wear off, don't I? To tell you the truth, I think I can sort of feel it happening now.'

Stacey and I peered at Bill closely. He definitely seemed to be getting hairier and some of his scales were coming off in the bath. And he appeared to be growing.

Stacey laughed and started to splash Bill. But I felt more than a bit put out. It didn't seem right that Bill was taking the situation so lightly. How was he so sure that he wasn't going to remain a cod–ugly fish for the rest of his life? As usual, it was up to me to sort out this mess. I sat down on the bathroom stool and started to rifle through the fish samples in my rucksack.

'These look the same as the stuff Dad normally sells,' I muttered, 'only the wrappers are a different colour. They're not very clearly labelled. ' I tore open a packet and squinted at its contents suspiciously. 'Nothing strange there,' I said, shaking it about. I sniffed it cautiously. It seemed to smell OK. I opened another bag. It was exactly the same. I laid both packets on the side of the bath while I rummaged around some more.

'Well, Bill, it looks as if you're right. There's nothing for it but to see what happens. We'll simply have to wait for you to turn back into a boy. I just hope it doesn't take too long. That bathroom lock still hasn't been mended – anyone could walk in. All I can say is thank goodness Mum's out. How long do you think it will be before she gets back?'

'Not long enough,' said Stacey, in a hollow voice, looking through the bathroom window. 'Guess who's walking up the garden path?'

'*Quick!*' I yelled to Stacey. '*Lock the door!*'

Stacey tried, but it was no good. The door lock was well and truly bust, and however much she tried to force it, it would not jam shut. Bill started to panic.

'NED! Ned! Help me!' he begged, dashing up and down the bath. 'Hide me! Put me somewhere! Mum will go mental if she sees me like this!'

'But where?' I cried, trying hard to keep calm. Bill had grown even bigger. 'I can't put you in the bucket, and you're too big to fit down the loo!'

'But she'll *kill* me if she catches me like this!'

'Well – maybe you should have thought about that before you started fooling around with Dad's fish food,' I snarled.

But Bill was right. Mum was going to explode. And not just with Bill. When she discovered that her youngest son had turned into a fish and played hide-and-seek with a killer whale in public, I reckoned I would be next in the firing line. She always seemed to think that it was my job to look after Bill. We were both well and truly kippered.

'Coo-ee!' trilled Mum from downstairs. 'I'm back! Is anyone at home?'

'Ssh!' I whispered. 'Don't say anything!'

We held our breath, but we reckoned without Mum's supersonic hearing.

'Oh, you're upstairs, are you?' she said. 'Well, just

hang on while I get the shopping in and then I'll come up and see you. I'm longing to show you my new hairdo!' We heard her put down her bags and go back outside to the car.

We were in a right kettle of fish. I shut my eyes and thought fast.

'Right,' I hissed, dragging up the stool. 'Stacey, you sit on this and lean against the door. Wedge your feet against the bath, and whatever you do don't let Mum in!' Before I could say anything else, I heard Mum starting to climb the stairs.

'Bill, Stacey, Ned!' she called. 'Where's Dad? What are you all doing in the bathroom? Are you OK? Did you have fun at the zoo? Did you manage to get rid of any T-shirts?'

No one said a word.

Mum instantly went on red alert. Her voice became much sharper. 'Ned, Stacey, Bill? What's going on?' She rapped on the door. 'Look,' she said, 'I know you're in there, so you might as well own up. What are you doing?'

'Er , nothing,' I said shakily. 'Bill's just having a bath …'

'Having a bath? Bill? At this time of day?' squawked Mum. 'He must be mad. It's all I can do to get him

to have one before bed. Are you sure he's OK?'
She rattled the door. Stacey's face was going bright
pink with the effort of pushing against it. 'And
what's wrong with the door? Why can't I get in?'

'Er, don't worry, Mum,' I said desperately, 'I think
the handle's a bit stiff. And Bill's fine.' I laughed.
'He just got a bit wet and … er …' I fished around
for some inspiration and saw Stacey's luminous
T-shirt, '… some of the dye came off his shirt, so
we're giving him a wash …'

I wiped my forehead. Sweat was dripping off me. I wasn't used to lying.

Mum was just about to answer when Dad arrived home.

'Dan! Dan!' hollered Mum from the other side of the bathroom door. 'Bill's having a bath and the kids are telling me some story about the dye coming out of Geoff's grotty T-shirts! What on earth's been going on? And the bathroom door's jammed. I've told you time and again about that door!'

Dad mumbled something and came upstairs.

He coughed loudly and said, importantly. 'Right, children, stand back! I'm going to thump the door hard a couple of times with my shoulder. If it still doesn't budge, I'll take a run at it from the end of the corridor. Don't panic, now. You'll be out any moment!'

Don't panic! *Don't panic!* Dad is over six feet tall. There was no way we could hold the door against him. I turned round to Bill.

'Dive!' I cried, pushing him under the water. But he had grown even bigger. The grey bulk of his cod–like form was clearly visible under the water. Desperate times require desperate measures. I grabbed a jar of Mum's favourite pink bubble bath and poured it under the running tap.

Stacey gasped, 'Oh, no! Not that one, Ned! It's Mum's favourite. It's called Pink Passion. It costs a fortune!'

'Well, if it hides Bill, then it will be worth its weight in gold!' I replied. I swirled the water round. Pink bubbles danced everywhere and clouds of scent filled the room.

Mum instantly smelt a rat – or should I say fish. She knocked hard on the door. She was no longer sympathetic, she was suspicious.

'Children! Children! What are you doing with my best bath oil? I can smell it from here – do you know how much it cost?'

We all ignored her. So did Dad.

'Stand clear!' he cried from outside, rolling up his sleeves and preparing for his first strike. 'I'm coming in!'

THUMP! went the door. Mum yelped. Bill ducked below the water and then bobbed up almost instantly.

'Yuck!' spluttered Bill, spitting pink bubbles everywhere. 'This stuff stinks! You can't possibly think I'm going to hide under this rubbish?'

'Yes, I do!' I hissed, shoving him back down under the water. 'This is the only chance we have of saving you from being fried alive by Mum and Dad!'

THUMP! Dad hit the door a second time.

'Ouch!' went Stacey, but she held firm.

I yanked the shower curtain round the bath and accidentally knocked the two open packets of fish food I'd balanced on the side of the bath. They shot up into the air, scattering their contents everywhere. Instantly, Bill – a sucker for free food even in a crisis – jumped out of the water and gobbled up the lot.

I stared at him, aghast. 'Bill, Bill what have you done now?' I wailed. Surely, not even my crustacean of a brother could have been so stupid as to eat a double dose of Dad's dodgy fish food? What was he going to turn into this time? An octopus?

Even Bill realised he'd been a bit silly. 'N-ee-d!' he said, in a faint voice. 'I don't feel very well. I've got a bit of a tummy ache. In fact, I think …' His voice trailed off. There was a flash! A bang! And a whizz! And somehow, some way, Bill-the-cod changed back into a boy. Where one moment there had been a large and ugly grey fish with a shock of yellow curly hair, there was now my brother, sitting up to his chin in pink bubbles, butt-naked and covered in gloopy grey slime!

'Bill! B–iii–ll's back!' sobbed Stacey, with relief.

I nodded in silence. I was too stunned to speak. How had Bill done it? How had he managed to turn himself back into a boy just like that? I fished out one of the empty crisp packets from the water and stared at it blankly. But before I could do any more, Dad rapped on the door.

'Now children,' he said, gravely, 'watch out! I'm going to take a run at the door from the end of the corridor! I don't want to hurt you, so stand clear!'

I shot another look at Bill. His hair was covered in greasy grey scales. Thinking quickly, I grabbed Mum's bright pink bath cap and rammed it over his head, just as Dad charged at the door. Caught off guard, Stacey toppled forward off the stool, and Dad and Mum fell into the room.

'Ah, I knew that would do the trick!' said Dad, carelessly, trying hard not to rub his shoulder. 'Just as I thought, the door was jammed ...' His voice trailed off as he saw Bill. He was sitting bolt upright in a sea of pink bubbles, wearing Mum's fluffy pink bath cap and covered in what looked like ghoulish-grey face paint.

'What on earth ...?' he spluttered, looking at his youngest son. There was silence. Then Mum spoke. 'Bill, darling, what have they done to you?'

'*US?*' Stacey squealed, unable to stand the injustice of it all. 'What have WE done to *HIM*?'

'Erm, don't worry, Mum,' I interrupted, hastily. 'That grey stuff's just one of Stacey's face masks. Bill was experimenting.' I lowered my voice. 'He thinks he's got spots – and another nit infestation,' I whispered confidentially.

Mum closed her eyes in horror.

'Spots!' cried Dad, whose eyes were out on stalks.

'And nits? But he's up to his neck in PINK BUBBLES!'

'It's the smell — and the colour,' I said, desperately. 'As of today, he really, *really* likes the colour pink.'

'Yeah, and the school nurse says that nits are particularly allergic to anything pink,' said Stacey, convincingly. She was enjoying this. 'And Bill, er, wants to get in touch with … with … his feminine side. I think he was inspired,' she said, warming to the theme, 'by your T-shirts, Dad.'

It was all too much for Dad. He gulped and sat down on the side of the bath. 'My T-shirts?' he whispered faintly. 'His feminine side? But he's only six …'

'Oh, well,' said Mum, regaining her powers of speech and trying to put a positive spin on matters, 'there's nothing wrong with pink, is there? After all, it's my favourite colour! Though next time, Bill, I think you should ask me before you use *all* my best bubble bath!'

Dad pulled himself together. 'Yes, yes, your mum's quite right, as always,' he said. 'Everything in moderation, that's what I say. Things have been really out of hand this past week. Why don't we all have a break? What do you say to all of us spending a bit of time together this weekend? We could go to the dogs? Or do some kick-boxing and perhaps even take in a rugby match?'

'Wicked!' cried Bill enthusiastically.

Stacey curled her lip in disgust – it's her automatic reaction to any suggestion that doesn't involve her friends, a make-up buying trip or a new magazine. I could only nod. I was too shattered to speak. All I knew was that there was no way I was going to tell Mum and Dad what had happened. Instead, I was just going to make sure it never happened again.

Which goes to show that even good plans can fail.

Chapter 13

FROM BAD TO WORSE

The rest of the weekend was almost normal.

After we had cleaned up Bill and dried out the bathroom, Mum and Dad insisted on us all doing things as a family. Stacey, who's read magazine articles about this sort of thing, told us this was called 'bonding' and refused to get excited. But Bill and I had a great time. First we went bowling, then we watched a football match on TV and on Sunday we played rugby at the local park all afternoon. Mum didn't complain once about our muddy boots, and even Stacey eventually said she enjoyed it (but only after Dad bought her a year's supply of Goopy Gloop Hair Spray and matching silver nail varnish). Nothing was said about the T-shirts, Bill's missing clothes and his non-existent spots (though Mum had a good look at his hair and found that he did indeed have nits). No one even mentioned the word zoo.

But every time I looked at my brother I had a terrible sinking feeling in the pit of my stomach.

I couldn't help wondering what Mum and Dad were going to say when they read all about us in the local newspaper. And what Dad would say if he really had lost his contract.

Bill, of course, was completely relaxed. 'It's cool!' he said, as we cleaned our teeth on Sunday night. 'There's *no Finn* to worry about!'

I nearly choked. Bill was becoming worryingly like Dad.

Stacey was a bit grumpier about it all. She had always wanted to be a star and was worried that she might miss this splendid opportunity for media exposure. 'I bet no one notices us,' she complained. 'It will be just *typical*! There'll probably be a poxy little paragraph tucked away on the inside back page. No one will notice us, no one!'

That sounded good to me. But unfortunately, both Bill and Stacey were wrong.

We were front page news.

screamed the headline. There was a huge picture of me standing on Stacey's ear, looking white-faced and exhausted. There was also a close-up of Bill in the bucket. I groaned.

Mum, who was eating breakfast when the local paper arrived, stared at it in disbelief.

'I've never read such a load of old codswallop,' she said finally. 'I can't believe you did all this for a fish,' she said. 'You hate them. Hang on.' She paused. 'Where's Bill?' There was silence. I scowled into my bowl of cereal and kicked Bill on the foot to keep him quiet. 'Do you know,' she said, studying the second picture more closely, 'I swear that fish looks a bit familiar ...'

Dad, of course, was thrilled. 'Well done,' he said, clapping me on the back. 'I'm proud of you. Saving a fish from a killer whale, eh! That's good stuff, especially,' he rubbed his hands, 'especially as you managed to get a picture of our T-shirts on the front page of the daily rag. It's excellent publicity. Especially now we've lost the contract to feed Kylie.' Dad had been very deflated by that news.

Donna had sent him a letter in that morning's post. Fortunately, she had not mentioned us.

But if home was tricky, school was even worse.

First of all, Dad insisted on walking with me across the playground, right up to the entrance. He clasped a copy of the newspaper to his chest making sure that the photograph faced outwards for everybody to see.

He kept referring to it in a cheery, breezy manner.

'Ah, Mr So-and-so, how are you? I'm just taking my son to school ... Seen the paper? No? Well, we don't want to brag about it, but he just happens to be on the front page ...' By the time I reached my locker, my face was as red as a lobster.

But school assembly was even more embarrassing.

'Ah, I see today that we have a hero in our midst,' said Mr Peaseby, our head teacher. He waved a copy of the paper in the air. 'On Saturday morning, young Ned Finn of P6 saved a cod from the jaws of a killer whale.' There was a murmur of admiration. I went bright red. Then Mr Peaseby pointed to me and said, 'Now, now, come on, Ned. Don't be shy. Why don't you stand up and tell us all about it?'

I struggled to my feet. Somehow I managed to give an (extremely edited) version of events. But that wasn't enough for Mr Peaseby.

'Well done, Ned! Well done!' he exclaimed. 'But before you sit down, tell us. Who thought up the design for those pink T-shirts? That lime-green swirly writing is just the ticket.' He looked hard at the photograph. I tried to ignore the sniggers around me. 'You see, I think they're rather cool.'

I blinked. Mr Peaseby obviously shared Dad's fashion sense. 'I mean, look at this joke – *"Just say Moo!"* ' He laughed heartily. 'It's brilliant! Perfect for Mrs Peaseby's birthday present. In fact, I'll even get one for myself. Do you think I could buy a couple? How much do they cost?'

My head spun. Could he be *serious?* Could anyone really want to pay good money for Dad's grotty gear?

But before I could answer, Bill – always a number cruncher piped up. 'Six pounds plus two pounds post and packaging with a discount for orders over five.'

'Well, I'll take two,' smiled the head. 'Anyone else interested?'

To my amazement, a forest of hands went up. I couldn't believe it. We were in business. We were making money. This was great!

Then one hand went up that I wish I had not seen.

It was Joe Blagg.

'Please, sir, can I ask a question?' he asked thickly, through a mouthful of sweets.

'Er, yes, I suppose so, Joe. What is it?' queried the head, nervously running his finger around his collar.

'Well, sir, I was thinking that instead of going through all the heats to decide who should represent the school at next week's Inter-School Quiz Championship, why don't we just ask Ned? Seeing that he's so brave and clever and all that! In fact, I have it on good authority that he's been secretly swotting in his room ... or should I say, *study?*'

My jaw dropped. *Stacey!* I thought. *Trust* her and her wretched mobile phone. Couldn't we have any secrets in our family any more? I glared at my sister. She went bright pink and avoided my gaze.

Joe, smiling smugly, continued, 'We could invite the local press along too. It would be great publicity for the school! So it wouldn't even matter if he didn't do that well. Just think of the headlines: "Cod Hero is Quiz King!" ' He paused to let the force of his words sink in. 'In fact, if you like,' he continued in a reasonable voice, 'I could ring Dad on my mobile and ask him to talk to a few journalists today. He's very friendly with journalists.'

That was true. They were constantly ringing him up to check on his dodgy car deals.

There was silence. The school quiz! I had completely (well, almost completely) forgotten about it. Winning the TOL3, PlayStation, surround-sound cinema and plasma screen TV suddenly didn't seem that important. I hadn't looked at a book for two days and I couldn't remember a single fact. Surely Mr Peaseby would tell him it was a rubbish idea? I tried to keep calm, but all I could feel was the knocking of my knees and the thumping of my heart.

'Ah, yes, Joe,' said Mr Peaseby, tugging nervously at his bow-tie. 'But, you know, Ned needs a special subject. And it's hardly fair to land one on him at such short notice.' He looked away, glad to be able to dismiss the idea.

But Joe wasn't being put off that easily. 'Surely, sir,' he said pleasantly, looking directly at me with evil eyes which showed just how deep his jealousy was, 'Ned could simply talk about his family's favourite hobby? Nits and nit-picking!'

There was a stunned silence and then everyone in the hall burst out laughing. Even the head teacher allowed himself a smile. But Stacey and I, sticking together once again through thick and Finn, silently vowed to get even with our enemy, Joe. How *dare* he take pot shots at our family? Just because Bill's head was the nits' equivalent of Heathrow Airport, that did *not* make me an expert on them! I glared at Joe's smirking face, but before I could do anything, the head teacher coughed, struggling to make himself heard above the din.

'Ah, yes, Joe,' he said rather pompously, 'I see you are talking about our great friend the head louse, or, as we should say in Latin: the *Pediculus Humanus Capitus.*' He chuckled to himself, pleased that he had been given a chance to show off his knowledge. 'As you know, they are extremely common, especially in school children. According to a recent survey, approximately seven per cent of a community will have head lice at any one time, with six- to twelve-year-olds being the most common sufferers. For some reason, like threadworms, infestations tend to happen …'

And with that he was off, droning on and on about lice, threadworms, slap-cheek, warts, verucas

... dandruff ... Our eyes started to glaze over and, for all I know, we might still have been sitting there now, listening to the lesser-known facts of in-growing toenails and athlete's foot, had Joe not decided to take matters back into his own hands.

He coughed. 'Oh, sorry, sir,' he apologised greasily. 'Of course, I didn't mean nits – I mean, it wouldn't be *fair* to blame the *whole* school's problems on Ned and his younger brother Bill ...' It was now Bill's turn to glower at Joe. 'Oh, no, sir! I didn't mean nits, I meant *knitting*. Ned's mum's a dab-hand at knocking up those weird – I mean, wonderful – jumpers and socks. I'm sure he'll be able to tell us a load of old balls ... I *mean about* all her balls of wool!'

There was another burst of laughter and, once more, everyone started to clap. The head teacher, surprised by the sudden and unexpected turn of events, smiled and nodded in agreement.

'Well done, Joe,' he gushed. 'Knitting is an excellent subject!'

And so the assembly ended and everyone sidled out of the hall. I couldn't wait to get out of there. I was in a fix. What did I know about knitting? Or care for that matter? No, I was in a right old tangle, complete with knots and frayed ends. There was no casting off for me, that was for sure. I knew only one thing: that if ever I hated fish, I hated them now.

Chapter 14
SOLE BROTHERS

It was my brother who sorted it out. He was the sole of resourcefulness.

'Don't worry,' he said confidently, 'I can help you.'

'*You?*' I said rudely. 'How?'

Bill did a double backflip. We were back in the bathroom. My brother, currently in the shape of a fish, was showing off. Stacey and I were sitting on the edge of the bath, watching his latest performance.

'It's easy,' he said confidently. 'I have a plan.' I stared at my brother uneasily. Somehow, whatever this plan was, I didn't think I was going to enjoy my part in it very much. 'You see,' continued Bill happily, 'I've worked out exactly how to turn from a boy into a fish and back again using Dad's formula … Only, it's not my discovery, exactly. I got the idea from one of

Stacey's science books over there.'

Stacey and I both stared in amazement at a pale blue exercise book that was half hidden under her overflowing bag of make-up. It was smudged with glittery pink nail varnish and decorated with purple love hearts and hundreds of dramatic signatures saying 'Stacey Pitt' and 'Stacey Depp'. It didn't instantly look the kind of book in which you might uncover an earth-shattering scientific discovery.

Stacey looked sceptical. 'Are you sure?'

'Oh, yes. Positive! It's a fascinating book, Stacey. You should read it sometime!' Bill, who I had to remind myself, was only six, then started to spout out a whole series of number-crunching formulae. I still don't have a clue what he was going on about, so I've jotted down a few of them just in case they might make some sense to someone else.

Stacey and I listened to our brother in mounting awe.

'Do you know,' Stacey breathed in respect, 'Mum and Dad are right. If you spent half a moment concentrating in class, you could be running the school by now!'

'Yes, but just imagine how dull life would be! I would never have time to do any of this!' cried Bill, leaping in and out of the water. He caught sight of my blank face and started to swim up and down the bath. 'I LOVE being a fish! It's such fun and it doesn't hurt a bit! In fact, the only annoying thing is not being sure what will happen to my clothes. Sometimes I change back stark naked! Just imagine if someone was passing by. It could be very embarrassing!' He laughed, but stopped when he saw the blank look on my face.

'Look, Ned,' he said patiently, 'this fish-changing business is really very simple. If I eat two packets of Dad's Super-Strong Fish Crisps, I change into a cod. If I eat another two, I change back. If I hold my breath and count backwards for the next five seconds I stay small; if I blow outwards, I become huge – well, bigger than I am now. It's easy, really,' he added modestly. 'If I take a risk and don't eat any extra fish food, then I eventually do turn back into a fish, but it takes longer and longer each time and it does leave me smelling a little bit fishy …'

I had noticed he was whiffier than usual, come to think about it. I had put it down to Mum's anti-nit shampoo.

Intrigued, Stacey and I decided to test out Bill's theory. And it turned out that Bill was right. It took exactly two packets. Too little and he ended up as a fish with yellow hair; too much and he ended up as a boy with fins. Each time he changed, there was a flash! A bang! And a whizz! But it never seemed to hurt him, however many times he did it. Thankfully, Dad's other fish crisps – the ones for use in homes and aquariums – had no effect on Bill at all. When he munched those, Bill stayed exactly the same – a rather annoying, awkward boy.

I sighed uneasily. 'This is all very well, you know, but it's not going to stop me making an utter fool of myself in the Quiz.'

The whole school knew that Joe had bet all his parents' holiday cash on me to fail. But it wasn't just the money. Joe had been going round bullying everyone to make sure they didn't help me. His impersonation of a human sledgehammer was not a pretty sight.

Bill smiled from the bath. 'Don't worry,' he tried to reassure me. 'I've told you – I have a cunning plan.'

Just at that moment the doorbell rang. Bill, swallowing exactly the right quantity of Super-Strong Fish Crisps, swiftly turned back into a boy, and tidied up the bathroom whilst Stacey and I ran to the banisters to see who was there. Mum opened the door, and we all had a shock. There, wearing huge sunglasses and hiding behind a large, ragged and strangely familiar-looking bunch of flowers, teetered Ms Donna Mezzweme, the Marine Life Manager from the zoo.

'Ah, Mrs Finn, I presume,' she said, thrusting the flowers into Mum's hands. 'These are for you.'

'Thank you,' our mother spluttered. Donna Mezzweme swept past her into the front hall. She smiled, or at least tried to. Somehow it looked like a rather nasty grimace

'I wouldn't get too excited by them.' Her laugh was chilling. 'I found them in your front garden. I always think hand-picked flowers are the best, don't you?' Without waiting for Mum to answer, she dramatically swept off her sunglasses and started to tap the toe of one of her high-heeled shoes on the floor.

'Hmm, just as I thought,' she said, looking around the room. 'Scruffy and unkempt – I mean *fluffy* and *well kept*, Mrs Finn!' she recovered, and went on. 'You might, Mrs Finn, be wondering why I have bothered to visit you in this dump – I mean, in your charming house.' She looked round the hall, curling her lip. 'Well, I am here to personally congratulate your delightful children on their wonderful act of bravery – and to see their cod! EVERYONE is asking about them. EVERYONE wants to see that fish. So, WHERE are the brats – I mean sprats? And, more importantly –' she broke off and thrust her nose straight into Mum's face through the flowers, 'WHERE is that *cod*?'

Mum, who had also been trying to winkle this information out of us, was taken by surprise. Flustered and struggling hard to be polite, she stammered, 'W—well, the children are upstairs, I think … but I don't know if their fish is —'

'No matter,' cried Donna Mezzweme, heading for the staircase. 'If that fish is in the house, I'll sniff it out.'

Upstairs, Bill, Stacey and I gasped. What were we going to do? We didn't have a cod, let alone one we could give to Donna. The only cod we knew had two legs, a head and no tail and was currently crouched beside me in the shape of my brother, Bill.

It was too late to think of anything, for at that moment Donna Mezzweme tripped over us and fell flat on the ground. She had put her dark glasses back on and hadn't noticed that we were huddled by the banisters.

'What the —?' she spluttered furiously, scrabbling up on to her hands and knees.

She glared malevolently. 'I should have known it would be your fault,' she snarled. 'Goodness, how I *hate* children. Now,' she said, grabbing me by the ear, 'if you know what is good for you, SHOW ME THAT COD!'

'Er, it's in the ornamental pond, in the garden,' I blurted out with what I thought was a stroke of genius.

'Well, take me there at once!' retorted the enraged Donna, letting go of me.

We stood up, but something caught Donna's eye. It was the notice on my old (now Stacey's new) bedroom door. Stacey, stubborn to the last, had defied Mum and refused to take it down. The Marine Life Manager went over and read it closely.

'Hoooow interesting,' said Ms Mezzweme. 'Fish farmers, eh? Super-Strong Fish Crisps for ...' she caught her breath, '*Scarce Sea Fish* ... Then THIS notice must refer to an important new type of fish food – one that Dan – your Dad,' she smiled gushingly at us, 'HAS JOLLY WELL FORGOTTEN TO TELL ME ALL ABOUT! Hah! We'll see about that. Now SHOW ME YOUR ROOM!'

We had no choice. Donna flung open the door, strode in, and tripped a second time, slap into a pile of my dirty underwear and unwashed socks.

'Yeuch!' she cried, scrabbling about. 'Help! Get me out of here!'

We couldn't, even if we had wanted to. We were laughing too much. Furious, Donna tried to scrabble her way back to her feet. But the heels of her shoes had become trapped in the neck hole of one of my vests, and she fell over again as soon as she stepped forwards. Angry and humiliated, she started chucking pants, vests and socks at us. One sock landed on the lampshade, another vest on my bunk bed. By the time she reached my cupboard she was out of breath and had broken two of her bright red talons. That didn't stop her trying to prise open the cupboard door, despite the fact that it was jammed right against the bunk beds, just as Dad had intended. Shaking with rage, she started kicking the cupboard and thumping the door with her hands. She was making such a terrible noise that Mum came pounding up the stairs.

'And just what,' she said in a voice that could cut ice, '*exactly* do you think you are doing, Ms Mezzweme? And why do you have a pair of Ned's dirty underpants hanging from your sunglasses?'

Donna was disconcerted. 'Oh, er, nothing – I was just looking for the cod!' she stuttered.

'Well, I *don't* think you'll find it in there!' rapped my mother, coming to our rescue. Making an inspired guess, she continued, 'I think you'll find it in the garden in the ornamental pond! Stacey, Ned, take Miss Messypants into the garden *at once* – she can leave by the side gate.' And with that she nodded curtly to the Marine Life Manager, turned on her heel and left the room.

There was an awkward silence. Stacey politely beckoned Ms Mezzweme down the stairs and we trooped out into the garden in silence. I hung well back. My ear was still throbbing from where she had twisted it. Bill had disappeared. I didn't blame him one bit.

The grass around the pond was wet and muddy. Ms Mezzweme's shoes sank into it, leaving large holes wherever she walked. Soon, her shoes were caked with earth and grass. The manager was not impressed.

'Eeuch!' she screeched. 'If there's one thing I hate more than children, it's nature! Hasn't anyone in this house heard of decking and concrete?'

We ignored her and reached the pond. I peered down. There, lying next to Goldie-the-goldfish, was Bill-the-cod! Using that brilliant brain of his, Bill had secretly eaten some of Dad's Super-Strong Fish Crisps and turned into a cod in order to help us out. I could have hugged him!

I pointed Bill out to Miss Mezzweme. 'Look, there's the cod, just by the lily pad,' I said.

Grumbling, Donna Mezzweme bent down carefully. Bill took aim and 'Thwack!' he jumped out of the water and hit her straight in the eye. Donna jumped back in alarm and, as she did so, we all heard the tell tale ripping of her rather tight skirt.

'Owwwwwwwwwwwww! That does it! I've had it!' stormed Donna indignantly. 'I only came here to buy your blasted cod. *Some* people,' she hissed, 'are saying that Kylie's bored and that I should make her life more *fun!* Of all the ridiculous ideas!' she sniffed. 'I mean, let's face it, Kylie's a killer whale, not a cuddly toy! I told them that their precious cod would be eaten in two seconds flat, but no, they tell me that Kylie is different, Kylie is sensitive, Kylie is a Hollywood star and just wants someone to play with ...'

There was a tense silence as Donna seemed to struggle for words. 'I mean, imagine − someone with my international reputation being asked to make sure that that great ball of blubber has some fun!' She tossed her hair backwards over her shoulder in disgust − her bun had completely fallen apart.

Stacey and I looked at each other, horrified at this monstrous woman who was obviously interested only in money and fame. Then the blood in our veins froze as she continued, more quietly but with an edge of evil in her voice.

'If you ask me, there was something very fishy about that fish. If you ask me ...' There was a pause as she eyed us strangely. 'And exactly *where is* your brother Bill?' We blinked blankly at her but she knew she was on to something. There was a further pause while Stacey and I swallowed hard, before Donna Mezzweme said, 'Hmm. Can't answer, can you? Well, don't worry, *I'll* find out!' Then she turned on her muddy heel, swept out of the side gate and started up her car.

Which was unfortunate, because at that moment, Dad drove at some speed into the yard.

Donna, who wasn't concentrating, drove straight into the wall to avoid him. There was a bang, a crash, a thud and a tinkle as her car fell apart around her. Donna was uninjured, but her car was a complete and utter write-off.

Mum, trying to hide her satisfaction, hurried out to help. 'I know just where you can find a replacement! Try Mr Blagg. He's well known round here – in fact he's got quite a reputation.'

And that's how Donna Mezzweme came to buy the cheapest and dodgiest car she could from the cheapest and dodgiest car dealer in town. And while she was there, guess what? She overheard Joe Blagg discussing his bet that I would lose the Inter-School Quiz Championship with his dad.

Donna, who had been face down in my dirty underwear, walloped by a cod and had demolished her car in our driveway, was desperate to get her own back. As keen as ever to make a quick buck, she eagerly put all her spare cash on me losing the competition.

When I heard this – Joe dropped it casually into the conversation at breaktime one day – I felt sicker than ever. Bill reassured me once again. But I still wasn't convinced by his plan.

'Don't worry,' he said. 'It will be easy. I'll turn into a fish and then you can take me into the quiz in a fishbowl as your lucky mascot. The girls will all have their fluffy Beanie babies and lucky shells, believe me. I've got a great memory. If you help me learn the facts, I'll be able to whisper the answers to you from the bowl. No one will suspect a thing. Nothing can go wrong.'

I had to admit that it was a brilliant plan. Bill had the best memory of anyone I knew. If he could help me, I had a real chance of winning the quiz. Yes, strictly speaking, we would be cheating, but what choice did we have? At least this way, we would defeat that bully Joe Blagg and get our own back on Donna Mezzweme. Everyone would be grateful – and no one would ever guess the truth.

Which just goes to show that whilst I knew little about fish, I knew even less about humans.

Chapter 15

DOUBLE SPEAK

The day of the Inter-School Quiz Championship dawned bright and cheery.

I felt about as cheery as a tin of pilchards.

My last hope – that Mum and Dad would ban me from being in the quiz when they heard that the first prize was a TOL3, PlayStation, and surround-sound home cinema system – came to nothing. Far from being disapproving, they were thrilled. It was just typical. There was I in urgent need of a bit of harsh, undeserved Victorian discipline (such as being banned from taking part in the competition by rigid, humourless parents who disapproved of any form of fun) when said parents promptly underwent a total attitude by-pass. I couldn't believe it! After banging on and on about how television and computers were the twin evils of our modern age, here they were promising me their full support and telling me (repeatedly) how brilliant I was even to have had the guts to enter the quiz.

In fact, this is what Dad said:

If-you-win-I'll-surf-the-internet-for-a-fishy-game-and-let's-have-a-bit-of-quality-time-together.

Mum was even worse!

Don't-worry — I'm-really-looking-forward-to-watching-educational-documentaries-with-you-on-your-surround-sound-home-cinema.

If you ask me, it was a classic case of PA (Parental Amnesia) or DS (Double Speak) — my term for the chasm between what parents say their offspring are to do and think, and what they then actually say, do and think themselves.

Now, I have done some research amongst my

friends and apparently PA/DS syndrome affects all parents, but my parents are definitely gold medallists in the sport. In fact, it affects them *so* badly and is *so* irritating that, if you don't mind, I am just going to take time out here to explain why I think it should be banned. *(On the other hand, if you want to skip on to the next bit of the story and miss out my rant, just hop to page 129 and I'll see you there!)*

PARENTAL AMNESIA OR DOUBLE SPEAK (PADS)

PADS Classic Example Number One: FOOD

What parents say:

1. Do not graze or eat between meals.
2. Do not taste food whilst you are cooking.
3. Always eat the food on your plate, including the vegetables.

What parents do:
1. Every time they go into the kitchen, they open the fridge door and (absent-mindedly) cut a chunk of cheese for themselves (Mum), or nibble at a bit of left-over lunch (Dad).
2. When cooking, Mum and Dad always taste the food.
3. On Christmas Day or at Gran's, Dad never eats his Brussels sprouts. He feeds them to the dog instead. So does Mum.

ACTUALLY, I MUST ADMIT... I'M NOT TERRIBLY KEEN ON THEM EITHER...

Ring any bells? Well, if not, try my second example, which is even more sinister.

PADS Classic Example Number Two: SUNBATHING

What parents say:
1. Don't go into the sun – or only if smothered in total block suncream.
2. Always wear a hat.
3. Only wear sensible clothes with long sleeves and legs.

What parents do:
1. Rush into the sun and lie stretched full out on the deck chair, ignoring all shade and wearing little or no suncream. By the end of the first day they look like lobsters.
2. Refuse/forget to wear their hats – and then drape their heads with towels or (if desperate) handkerchiefs when the heat has burnt their foreheads.
3. Wear as little as possible, which is a

pily as peeling red skin is not a pretty sight.

See what I mean? But do parents realise they have a problem? Will they admit it? Would they believe it even if we told them? No, of course not – and why? Because of their completely unfounded and totally unfair belief in the unwritten rule that:

**Parents Are Always Right
EVEN (or ESPECIALLY)
when they are WRONG**

WELCOME BACK
TO THOSE WHO SKIPPED THAT LAST BIT

Which is why – to get back to the story (and with apologies for my little aside) – I was so cross. It didn't matter how much I reminded them of their previous comments. The more I protested, the more Mum and Dad backtracked.

It was so perverse. I mean, if I couldn't even rely on my parents to be the unjust killjoys they normally were, what was the world coming to?

With these thoughts, and Mum and Dad's relentlessly cheery goodwill weighing heavy on my heart, I sank into the deep gloom of the doomed.

Bill, however, remained upbeat and perky.

'No worries!' he breezed cheerily, as he changed into a cod and plopped into the waiting fishbowl. 'I've been listening to you and Mum trying to swot up on knitting facts. The only difference between us is that I remember everything and you don't remember anything! Just carry me along to that hall and I'll whisper you the answers.'

But something told me it was not going to be as easy as all that.

And whatever that something was, it was right.

Chapter 16
THE SCHOOL QUIZ

The school hall was already packed when we arrived. Joe Blagg and his family had kept their promise and done their worst. I was finished. Everywhere I looked, I could see the happy smiling faces of important-looking guests. Mum was dead impressed and kept pointing them out with her number ten knitting needles. There were the members of the press, the managers of local stores and football clubs, the school governors, visiting head teachers, the mayor and mayoress – even, sitting all alone in a corner, the wretched Donna Mezzweme.

But what really thrilled Mum was that some of my supporters had decided to wear Dad's hideous

T-shirts in honour of the event. Had they no taste? In fact, it was all Stacey and I could do to prevent Mum and Dad rushing home to get some more T-shirts to meet the demand before the quiz started.

Everyone seemed in a carnival mood; everyone was having fun; everyone was looking forward to a keenly fought match.

Except for me.

I was perched on the edge of a chair clutching Bill's bowl to my chest, trying not to panic. My stomach was in knots. My palms were sweaty and I could feel my hair sticking to the nape of my neck. Bill, on the other hand, was as confident as ever. He was splashing about in the water as though he didn't have a care in the world. As for Stacey, she was cramming her face with cake and commenting rudely and audibly on the other contestants. There were about sixteen of them, all milling around the orange juice table trying to act cool. Suddenly, she gasped in dismay.

'Uh oh, look what the cat's dragged in,' she hissed angrily. 'Princess Perfect and her brother Einstein.

Izzy warned me about them.' She sighed and shook her head with frustration. 'I thought they were on holiday, but they must have come back early to take part in the competition! Well, bro, I'm afraid to say it, but I think you're stuffed!' And as if to prove her point, she quickly demolished her third chocolate éclair. Speaking thickly through a mouthful of chocolate and cream, she continued, 'Those twins win *everything*. They're the brainiest people on the planet! *She's* the head prefect of that stuck-up school in the middle of town and he's at that school for gifted freaky boys at the other side of the ring road. You haven't got a chance! According to Izzy, Einstein's so bright he actually knows every single answer in Trivial Pursuit – including the anniversary edition!'

This was all I needed. The Princess was indeed the Perfect Prefect – gracious, glossy and well-groomed. Even her white, knee-length socks looked as if they were standing smartly to attention without a single wrinkle. Behind her, faultlessly sorting out a Rubik's cube, walked her tall, geeky-looking twin. One glance at this Brainbox Duo and I knew that we were sunk. And if we weren't going to win, we might as well pack up and go home – why prolong the agony?

Sighing with relief, I was just about to make my move when Stacey gave a second gasp. Struggling for breath, she seized my arm with such a vice-like grip that I almost dropped Bill's bowl.

'*Oi!*' yelled my brother indignantly as water splashed on to the floor.

'Ssh!' hissed Stacey. 'Be quiet or he'll see you!'

'*Who?* Who will?' said Bill, leaping frantically out of the water. But Stacey wasn't listening. Instead she had jumped up and was squirming around on her tiptoes, frantically trying to swallow her last piece of cake and spluttering crumbs everywhere. I followed her gaze – and saw exactly what she and every other girl in the room was looking at: Mikhail Sportanovitch, our neighbouring school's very own heart-throb.

His fans – every single girl in our school – call him *The Dude*. Bill and I call him The Dud. We feel that's a more accurate description.

I groaned. 'Oh no, Stacey. Please tell me you're not still mad about that loser?' I begged. 'He's a complete waste of space!'

Stacey was just about to launch a blistering defence of her hero when Bill decided to stick in his fin's worth too. He considered his sister carefully through the glass and said, 'Do you know, Stacey, you've gone bright pink? It must be all that cake. I wouldn't let him see you like that – pink really clashes with your bright red –'

'If you say *hair* I for one shall personally feed you to the nearest cat!' spat Stacey.

'All right, Goldilocks! Keep calm! I was actually referring to your spots!' retorted Bill huffily.

Stacey lunged furiously at Bill's bowl. Once again, I only just managed to keep a grip on it.

'Will you stop it?' I growled at my siblings. 'I'm about to die out there and all you can do is trade cheap personal insults!' Honestly, I thought I was about to have a fit. Luckily, before I did either of them grievous bodily harm, the head teacher bustled up, looking grim. Judging from his face, he too was having second thoughts about having Ned Finn representing the school's intellectual elite. Seizing me by the wrist, he insisted on checking my pulse, which was racing.

'Ah hah!' cried Mr Peaseby triumphantly. 'Just as I thought. The boy is over-stressed. No wonder, with all he's gone through recently. Withdraw, dear boy, withdraw. Let someone else take your place.'

He smiled and looked up. He was just about to summon Ike Pearson, the school swot (Special Subject: *The Ten Best Head Teachers of Brackenbridge School* and *How to Spell the One Hundred Longest Words in the Dictionary Backwards*) to take my seat, when he found himself confronted by Joe Blagg's mother clutching her nasty-looking handbag.

'What's wrong with the snotty little squit, then?' she demanded.

The head shuffled his feet. 'He's, ah, got a headache – sadly – and is feeling rather faint. I think it might be wise to send him home. I'll just go and fetch his parents.' He tried to inch away from Mrs Blagg, but only succeeded in bumping into her equally ferocious husband.

'A little off-colour, is he?' demanded the car

salesman menacingly, thrusting his shiny red nose into Mr Peaseby's face. 'Maybe I should just give him a little once over, then, just to check that he's all right? Unless,' he paused, taking a large spanner out of his pocket and gently tapping it against Mr Peaseby's arm, '*unless* what you're telling me is a load of old tripe?'

The head teacher, completely unnerved, threw in the towel.

'No, no, that won't be necessary,' he stuttered. 'I'm sure he's only suffering from nerves and the heat in the hall.' He turned to me and shook my hand.

'Right, Ned,' he said, 'you'll just have to do the best you can.' He looked grimly resigned to an afternoon of failure for the school. 'Good luck,' he said. 'And be careful with that bowl.'

I sighed and struggled to my feet. I couldn't blame him for trying to replace me. I only wish he'd succeeded. With legs like lead, I made my way to join the other contestants. Competition monitors handed each of us a red cotton bib with a large black number on it. Mine was number thirteen. This was no coincidence. The monitor who gave it to me was Joe. I took one look at his smug smile and almost refused to put it on. But what was the point?

I trudged slowly up the steps to the platform. Three of the other contestants had taken their seats already:

1. The Dude a.k.a. Mikhail Sportanovitch (Special subject: Shot-Put Heroes of Brackenbridge School 1923– Present Day)
2. Princess Perfect: The Perfect Prefect (Special subject: Ironing Boards through the Ages)

3. Finstein (Special subject: The Kinematics of Uniform Circular Motion)

Smiling weakly at my rivals, I sat down and gingerly placed Bill on the table in front of me. Instantly, Joe's hand shot up.

'Sir, sir, excuse me, sir!' demanded the bully. 'What's Ned got in that bowl? How do we know he isn't cheating?'

A murmur rippled round the hall; press lights flashed. Mr Peaseby stood up and laughed genially.

'Now, now, Joe. You know very well that this is Ned's fish, his lucky mascot. We can hardly object to it.' I thought for one dreadful moment that he might add, 'After all, Ned needs all the help he can get.' I knew he was thinking that. But instead he paused and looked pointedly at the other pupils. 'Especially as everyone else has a mascot – even Mikhail Sportanovitch!'

It was true. In front of each contestant was a lucky charm. Einstein had his Rubik's cube (rumour had it that he trained his hands specially to twist it at spectacular speeds); the Perfect Prefect was fingering some Greek worry beads, and The Dud – or sorry, *Dude* – was fidgeting with a rather cumbersome rubber ball. He dropped it as soon as his name was mentioned, and it bounced all over the floor and finally fell off the stage. There was an unseemly scramble as a herd of she-elephants (led by Stacey) rushed to retrieve it. Blushing furiously, she finally emerged from the scrum dishevelled but triumphant, and coyly returned the ball to her hero.

I sighed. Bill was right. Stacey's pink face did clash badly with her red spots. Mikhail languidly pushed his fringe back from his eyes before raising the ball above his head like a trophy. There was a gasp of admiration from the girls, followed by a burst of applause.

Joe realised that his complaint had failed. Bill winked at me from the bowl (it seems that fish who have been boys can do this), and blew a few bubbles in mock relief. Then everyone settled down. There was a short silence and the quiz began.

At first the questions were easy. Each was drawn at random from a box with hundreds of cards in it. Apparently a group of retired teachers met every

Wednesday evening in the pub to think them up. We wrote our answers down in batches of five and handed them to the head teacher at the end of each round. The contestant with the least correct answers had to leave the platform. I survived the first eleven rounds and saw the expressions on the faces of my friends and family change from sympathy to surprise.

By the twelfth round, there were only a few of us left, and the questions had become much much harder. Of course I hadn't a clue what the answers were. I was only there courtesy of Bill, and so far our plan had worked. I would pretend to look very studious when in fact I was staring at Bill's fishy lips. Then, hunched low over my paper, I would scribble down his reply whilst my ear was glued next to the bowl, his tiny voice confirming what I had lip-read. We'd rehearsed our technique for hours and to begin with, all went well. No one suspected a thing. But then:

1. **Bill started to get bored.**
2. **Joe started to get suspicious.**

It all started when The Dud took three minutes to answer question nineteen. It was a maths problem.

This stumped him. So far only his encyclopaedic knowledge of sport and a big dollop of good luck had carried him through. Now, however, he was scuppered. There was a tense silence as The Dud rolled his eyes and tried to work out the answer to the question (or, as Bill uncharitably whispered to me – the meaning of the question). As the seconds ticked by, Bill decided to lighten the atmosphere by jumping out of the water a couple of times. Someone in the audience tittered. Encouraged, he did a backflip ... followed by a wheelie ... and then a double somersault.

By now everyone in the room was trying hard not to laugh. Their shoulders were shaking with stifled giggles. Spurred on by the attention, Bill performed a perfect triple somersault. The audience roared with approval, whistling and shouting for more.

The Dud was furious, but eventually he conceded defeat and swaggered off the stage muttering darkly about a conspiracy. There was a collective groan from his fan club and Stacey looked murderously at me and Bill.

'How *could* you?' she mouthed.

The head teacher gave me a stern stare and told me to control my bowl. I muttered to Bill to stay still, but he was enjoying himself far too much to stop.

'OK, OK,' he panted. 'Keep your scales on. Here's the deal.' He did a neat aquatic pirouette before facing me from the fishbowl.

'You have to let me have the top bunk and promise not to prod my bottom through the mattress, even if I wriggle about!'

Only my determination to wipe that smug smile off Joe's face kept me from grabbing that cod brother of mine by the gills and ... I nodded imperceptibly, and Bill swam off gracefully, mission accomplished. Gritting my teeth, but swearing privately to get even with my brother at the first opportunity, I settled down to concentrate on the rest of the quiz.

To be fair, Bill kept the correct answers flowing and it wasn't long before we were down to the last three contestants:

Princess Perfect
Einstein
and
the Finn Family Duo.

I suddenly had a vision of all that awesome equipment stacked in our living room. And of the look on Joe's face as I was left, the sole winner, on stage.

But we weren't in calm waters yet. Bill began to muck about. He took longer and longer to answer my questions. Instead, he would circle the bowl, stare in the opposite direction or float on his back blowing bubbles. I glared at him. But power had rather gone to Bill's scaly head. As part of his so-called 'new deal', I was now not only to give him the top bunk, I was also to:

1. Make his bed every morning.
2. Take his turn to unload the dishwasher.
3. Give him 70% of my sweet allowance – and 50% of my pocket money.
4. Take his turn to clear out the guinea pig's cage and change the cat litter.

5. Let him have my seat by the window on long car journeys, rather than telling him to sit in the middle because he is the smallest.
And ... worst of all ...
6. Have first turn of the TOL3, PlayStation and the surround-sound cinema system.

What choice did I have? My brother was holding me to ransom and I had no alternative but to give in to his demands. I had just reached the end of my tether (a request that I should *always* let him be banker in Monopoly – he cheats every time) when something unexpected happened. Princess Perfect, the Queen of Cool, made a series of mistakes and was forced to leave the quiz.

This was it! Ned versus Einstein! Somehow, some way, Bill and I had worked a miracle and reached the final countdown. Brackenbridge School was one step away from winning the Inter-School Quiz Championship. Bill and I were one step away from gadget heaven. And even better, Joe, the school bully, was one step away from his well-deserved comeuppance.

Bill, finally sensing the gravity of the situation, settled down and started to concentrate. The tension was electric. You could have heard a fish sneeze. Mr Peaseby, sweating slightly and as excited as anyone about the possibility of his school winning the Inter-School Quiz Championship for the first time in sixty-three years, stood up to ask the final question.

But Joe Blagg wasn't beaten yet. He realised that if I won this point then not only was he going to lose all his money, but so were his parents and half the school. He could contain himself no longer. His podgy pink fist shot up into the air.

'Sir, sir!' he cried impatiently, charging on to the platform. 'It's not fair. Ned is cheating! I know he is!'

There was uproar. Mr Blagg, who could see his ill-earned cash disappearing, had to be forcibly restrained by the football coach. Donna Mezzweme began to stamp her stilettos in fury. She had told anyone who would listen that she was ready to order a brand new sports car, just as soon as this wretched — or rather wonderful — competition was over. But now that it looked as though she would lose her money *and* be stuck with her useless car, she was not happy. Not happy at all.

Mr Peaseby, who was as surprised as anybody by my miraculous transformation from class idiot to top swot, was furious.

'Cheating! *Cheating?*' he thundered. 'And just how, Joe, do you think Ned cheated?'

'With this,' yelled Joe. He seized the fishbowl and held it above his head.

The head teacher blinked. 'Not that lucky mascot business again, Joe. You can't seriously expect me to believe that Ned is somehow being told the answers by a *fish*?' he exclaimed.

Someone sniggered in the audience. Cameras flashed. The journalists, scenting a good story, were scribbling furiously. Mr and Mrs Blagg shifted uncomfortably in their chairs.

But Mr Peaseby hadn't finished. He had been biffed by Mrs Blagg's handbag, threatened by her husband and bullied by her son too often not to savour the moment of their downfall. He took a deep breath and stroked his chin thoughtfully.

'Of course, Joe,' he continued, 'we do know that you and your family have bet a fortune against Ned winning the contest – wasn't it the money for your family holiday? So, obviously, you will be very concerned that you are going to lose it.' There was a tense silence. 'So, this is what we'll do. I'll put the fish here, on my desk where I can keep an eye on it. Ned,' he turned to me and pointed, 'will sit there at his desk. Dear me,' he chuckled gently to himself, 'I know that eating fish helps increase brainpower, but I never realised that listening to them could help you win a competition!'

There was a ripple of laughter from the audience, followed by a raucous cheer. Joe, red-faced and furious, stomped back to his seat. I started to sweat. This was the pits. Even Einstein looked uncomfortable.

Mr Peaseby cleared his throat. 'Right, you two!' he said sternly. 'Listen hard! This is the last question of the competition. Ned's special subject. If he answers it correctly, he will win the Inter-School Quiz Championship. Are you ready, Ned?'

I think I nodded. I can't remember now. My heart was hammering and there was a pounding noise in my ears. This was it. The final point. If I got this question right, Brackenbridge school would win the cup and we would get our TOL3 and all the other gizmos. But how could I, when Bill was so far away from me?

There was a deathly hush. I glimpsed Mum from the corner of my eye. She had abandoned her frantic knitting and was clutching Dad's arm as though her life depended on it. Stacey made a thumbs-up sign to me, and I noticed that both she and Izzy had their fingers, legs and arms crossed.

The head teacher cleared his throat. 'Right,' he said sonorously. I couldn't help feeling he was enjoying himself rather too much now. 'Here is the last question. I shall ask it only once. You will have exactly thirty seconds to make your reply. Think very carefully before you answer.' He paused and took a deep breath. 'In knitting, what kind of stitch would remind you of ...' he paused dramatically, 'an oyster?'

There was a tense silence. For one ghastly moment, my heart stopped still. I felt clammy and sick as the all-too familiar sense of panic welled up in my stomach. The seconds were ticking by: thirty, twenty-nine, twenty-eight, twenty-seven … My mind was a complete blank. *What kind of stitch? An oyster?* I stared frantically at Bill, but though he was jumping excitedly up and down out of his bowl, it was no good. I couldn't possibly hear his tiny voice from where I was sitting.

Suddenly, with only fifteen seconds left, the enormity of the situation dawned upon me. I had been cheating and now I was going to be caught out. Joe was going to win. I had lost my chance of revenge and it was all my own fault. How stupid could I get? Looking round the room at the sea of expectant faces, desperately willing me on, I felt nothing but a sinking sense of guilt and shame. How could I ever live this down? I had failed myself, my school, my family and my friends. The clock was still ticking − ten, nine, eight …

I stared numbly around and suddenly caught Mum's eye. And as soon as I saw her − *I remembered!* I couldn't believe it! I, Ned Finn, knew the answer! We were going to win the cup after all!

As the final seconds ticked away, I jumped up and screamed out the right reply: 'The purl!'

There was a deafening round of applause. Children

cheered (which was generous, considering so many of them were so out of pocket), teachers clapped each other on the back and my parents hugged each other with delight. Brackenbridge School had won; Joe Blagg had been made to look a fool, and the Blaggs and the beastly Donna Mezzweme had lost their money. Life could not get any better. Unless, that is, your name was Ned Finn, in which case you were one of two things: a dead hero or a live coward. Over the applause, I heard the unmistakable screech of the Marine Life Manager's voice:

'I want that fish!' she cried. 'Dead or alive! It is MY fish! It came from MY aquarium!'

I had no choice.

I grabbed Bill's bowl and decided to cut and run.

Unfortunately, so did Joe, Thrasher and Crasher. It was just like old times.

I headed for the boys' toilet block. Stacey and I had agreed that it was the best place to turn Bill back into a boy after the quiz. Joe, hot on my heels and an expert in toilet-bullying, pushed me towards the basins and slammed the door shut with his right foot.

'Right, you slimy little eel,' he snarled, grabbing my collar. 'Tell me how you cheated or I'll flush your fish down the pan!'

I took a deep breath. Winning was one thing; losing one's brother was quite another. I was about to confess to everything when there was a deafening yell. A toilet door burst open behind Joe and out shot Stacey, hurling toilet rolls. Thrasher and Crasher, who had just arrived at the scene, were so startled at seeing a girl in the boys' toilets that they tripped over each other and fell to the ground. Joe, equally surprised, let go of my collar. Then, realising his mistake, he lunged for the fishbowl. But he slipped on some soap and landed in a heap on top of his hapless henchmen.

'Let's go, Ned!' shouted Stacey.

I didn't need to be told twice. Without losing any more time, we rushed out of the toilets, down the corridor past startled groups of chatting parents and friends, out of the main door, through the school gates and straight for home. For the moment, we were safe.

But as I turned the corner on to the main road, I looked back over my shoulder and saw Joe. His fist was punching the air in fury and he was yelling just one word: '*Revenge!*'

Chapter 17
CODNAPPED!

As soon as we reached home, we hid Bill, still in his bowl, in the shade behind a large leafy plant. He was looking a little green after the force eight gale we'd created in his fishbowl as we ran home. Leaving Stacey to guard the back door, I raced up to his bedroom to get some packets of Dad's Super-Strong Fish Crisps from the box in my cupboard. Stacey had dropped our supplies when she grabbed all the toilet rolls, and we just had to hope that the cleaners would mistake them for the usual crisp packets when they cleaned the boys' toilets the following morning.

But when I went into the bedroom, I had a nasty shock. The room had been ransacked. The cupboard was lying on its side with its door wide open. It was completely empty. The box of Dad's secret fish food had gone. I couldn't find a single packet, however hard I searched. Instead, lying on the floor, I found a business card:

DONNA MEZZWEME

I ran to the window and called down to Stacey. When she came up and saw the devastated bedroom, she sat down on the bottom bunk, put her head in her hands and began to sob.

'What are we going to do now?' she cried. 'I mean, can Bill still turn back into a boy without the help of Dad's special Super-Strong Fish Crisps?'

I stared at her, speechlessly. We both knew the score. But just then, Mum and Dad appeared at the door. They had been running and were out of breath.

'I knew it!' said Dad, snatching the card from my hand. '*DONNA MEZZWEME,* my foot! That woman's a phoney. A crook! An industrial spy! *And* a master of disguise — that's why I didn't recognise her. She's no more a Marine Life Manager than I'm a T-shirt designer. I suddenly realised it when she began screaming the odds at the end of the quiz. Her real name is Madge Sprod. She was once a brilliant scientist, but she's now a notorious con-woman who makes her money by stealing other people's ideas and selling them to companies for vast sums of cash. She's always been after my experimental fish foods — even the ones for household pets. She's desperate for anything that will make her rich! And now that it looks as if I have hit upon a way of saving the world's fish stocks, she wants my formula more than ever! Who knows, she might even be working for that dastardly bunch of crooks, the Underwater Underworld. I've been told they'd stop at nothing to sabotage my attempts to restock the seas with fish!'

Dad sat down on the lower bunk next to Mum. Luckily he didn't put his head in his hands, as Mum's manically clacking knitting needles would have had an eye out. But I could tell that he was gutted.

'But Dad,' I cried, before I could stop myself, 'it's even worse than you think. She's stolen all your new fish food, so now we can't help Bill! He might be a fish for the rest of his life!'

Dad peered at me. 'Bill? A fish?'

I had let the cat out of the bag – or rather the fish out of the fishbowl.

Mum abruptly stopped knitting, the needles frozen in mid stitch. 'What do you mean – a fish? What's going on?'

I looked at Stacey. She nodded. It was time to tell all.

First we explained how Bill had become a fish. And then how he hadn't.

Next, we described Joe's jealousy and his challenge to me that I should represent the School in the Inter-School Quiz Championship.

After that, we forced ourselves to admit how we had cheated in order to win the contest. (It took quite a lot of squirming and wriggling to confess the truth.)

Finally, I described the fight in the boys' toilets and Joe's threat of revenge.

Mum and Dad listened to us in silence. Then Mum calmly put down her knitting and looked Dad straight in the eye.

'Dan, tell me the truth, is this possible? Could Bill have eaten your special Super-Strong Fish Crisps and turned into a ...' she had to force herself to say the word, '*cod*?'

Dad stood up and shifted uneasily from foot to foot, but answered truthfully. 'Yes, Petal, I'm afraid it could be. You see, when I invented my special formula for restocking the seas, we were given some new free chemicals to try out by a large company – probably the one that's now paying Donna What's-her-name as its spy! Well, the company promised me their stuff was safe and completely harmless. I thought it might improve our formula, so I tried it out. What a mistake! I've only used it so far in one of our recipes to strengthen the formula – and look what's happened! It's vital that we get our hands on the rest of these packets before anyone else changes shape! We must destroy them all. And I promise, I'll never, ever use an unnatural ingredient again!'

Mum nodded. 'Good idea!' she agreed, jumping up off the bed. 'Children, I think what you did was wrong, but I know you acted with the best of intentions. What we need to do is to sort out this problem, and fast. First, we must change Bill back into a boy. Luckily, I just happen to have a few extra samples of Dad's special formula fish food in my bag …' She delved into her bag of wool and brought out a carrier bag stuffed full of Dad's special fish crisps. 'Don't ask me why, but after Miss Fish Face's visit, I took some from the cupboard. I had a hunch that they might come in handy!'

We stared at her, open-mouthed. Mum is brilliant when things are tough. When she's in this kind of mood, nothing can stand in her way. We ran over and gave her a hug.

'Right,' continued Mum decisively. 'There's no time to waste! Donna will be on her way to the airport by now with Dad's crisps! We need to call the police. Ned, Stacey! You go and feed these crisps to Bill and change him back into a boy. Dad and I will go to the factory and destroy all the old formula and every single speck of the chemicals. This must never happen again!'

We nodded enthusiastically and ran downstairs, keen to introduce Mum and Dad to their new-looking son.

Except we couldn't, because Bill's bowl had disappeared.

All that was left was a badly written note.

IF U WanT
2 C your Fish
Again, Mete us at
the Akwarium
at the Zoo

Signed
The CODFATHER

Bill had been codnapped!

Chapter 18
REVENGE OF THE KILLER WHALE

I read the note carefully. It looked suspiciously like the work of Joe Blagg. I could tell his writing – a mixture of texting and bad spelling – anywhere.

Mum and Dad were brilliant. They drove us to the zoo in double quick time and then rushed back to the factory to destroy the dodgy formula and any remaining packets of that particular batch of fish crisps. Our job was to find Bill and to persuade Joe to give him back. Mum – our amazing, dynamic mum – had made herself crystal clear. We were not, under any circumstances, to do anything rash.

It was a pity, therefore, that in our haste to reach the aquarium, we did not notice the broken-down crock of a car by the side of the road. Its one careful lady owner was none other than that crook, Donna Mezzweme. (Madge, to her friends – so I shouldn't think anyone calls her that!) When she saw that we were heading for the zoo, she decided to sneak along and see what we were up to.

It was the end of the day and everyone was going home.

Everyone, that is, except for Joe and his two sidekicks Crasher and Thrasher.

Joe was holding the fishbowl. As soon as he saw us, he grinned and plunged his hand into the water.

'Look what I've got here,' he taunted, pulling Bill out and waving him about by the tail. 'It's your 'orrible little fish.'

Then, dropping Bill back into the bowl, he walked up to us and stuck his thickset jaw right into my face.

'Now look here,' he said, with breath that made kippers smell good, 'I don't know how you cheated and, quite frankly, I don't care. But I DO know that you cost me a lot of money and I want it back. So here's how it is:

161

'One, you tell me how you did it.

'Two, I tell the head.

'Three, he tells everyone else and gets them to give me my money back.

'Simple, ain't it? Right then,' he said, looking at me grimly. 'This is your last chance. 'Fess up or your fish cops it.'

And once again he plunged his podgy hand into the bowl and hauled out Bill.

I looked at my brother. Bill winked.

'Please, Joe –' I began. But Joe wasn't having any of it. Grunting at his henchmen, he heaved himself on to their shoulders and leant precariously over the side of the pool, dangling Bill by the tail.

'Cooee! Kylie!' he called. 'Nice fishy! Good killer whale! Come and see what Uncle Joe has got for you … A nice, tasty fish finger!'

Stacey nudged me in the back. Kylie was swimming backwards and forwards, her slim black fin slicing the water like a blade. Bill, however, seemed quite relaxed. I could almost swear that he was talking to Kylie – and then I remembered that, of course, he could! Hadn't Bill told Kylie a joke at their first encounter? I relaxed and looked my brother in the eye.

He winked a second time.

Joe was getting bored.

'OK, that's it,' he said angrily. 'I'll count to three. If you haven't told me your scam before I finish, then this floating dustbin can have her smelly snack. Right …' he said. 'One … two …'

And that's when it happened. Joe was just about to count to three, when Kylie's big black nose reared out of the water, bang in front of Joe Blagg's face.

'Aaagh!' screamed Crasher and Thrasher, letting go of Joe and running away.

'Aaagh!' screamed Joe, falling into the tank.

'Yippee!' laughed Bill, released from the bully's hand and diving into the aquarium. 'Isn't this fun!'

'Fun!' I spluttered. 'What happens if Kylie eats Joe?' For Kylie was chasing Joe around the pool, snapping at his ankles. But although it looked as though she was going to bite him each time, in the end she only bumped him with her nose.

Bill laughed. 'Don't worry. Kylie's only playing with him as revenge for me. I've told her what's been going on. Isn't it lucky that I can speak fish?'

Bill was born lucky. But I was not and what little luck I had was most definitely about to run out. I quickly fed Bill the two packets of Dad's Super-Strong Fish Crisps. With a whizz and a flash and a bang, he turned back into a boy. Then, ignoring my fear of water and going completely against my better instincts, I dived into the tank and rescued the worst bully the school had ever known. Stacey and Bill cheered loudly. With their help, I heaved Joe over the side of the aquarium and back on to dry land. Fat, wet, tired and thwarted, Joe lay sprawled across the ground, panting for breath.

Thrasher and Crasher were nowhere to be seen. It was time to go home.

But just then, I felt a tap on my shoulder.

'Ah, Ned,' said a horribly familiar voice that sent shivers down my spine. 'It's Donna Mezzweme here. You know, the (former) manager of the aquarium, the (FUTURE) star of Hollywood and the (presently) broke punter with a CLAPPED OUT CAR!' She coughed and regained her composure. Her long, scarlet talons rested on my sleeve. 'Well, if you don't mind, I wonder if you could tell me just EXACTLY WHAT IS GOING ON?'

Chapter 19
WINNING THE CATCH

I spun round and stared at her in a panic. If Bill had turned back into a boy in front of Donna Mezzweme she must have seen everything! What on earth were we to do?

Luckily, before I could answer, Dad and Mum rushed up.

'Hah! Ms Donna-Madge-Sprout, or whatever your name is!' snarled Dad, looking most un-Dadish. 'I see you're up to your rotten tricks again! Well, this time, *this* time, I'm going to call the police!'

'You wouldn't dare!' Donna sneered, peering down at him from over her glasses. 'For if you did, *I* would have to tell them all about your fishy crisps – and,' she paused and looked at Bill, 'YOUR

EVEN FISHIER SON!'

Mum groaned and clutched Stacey to her chest. I think she was looking for comfort, but as she had a pair of knitting needles sticking out of the top of her jacket pocket, all Stacey felt was a jab in the chin.

The pain seemed to galvanise Stacey into action. It hurts me to say this after all she'd put me through, but I was proud of my sister. She turned and squared up to the former zoo boss.

'Look, Donna Trout!' she said, stepping deliberately on the woman's foot, 'I don't know who you are or why you're here, but I *do* know that you are a thief and a crook and that ...' and she took a deep breath, 'I ABSOLUTELY CANNOT STAND YOU!'

And with that she grabbed Donna's hair. It was a wig – and a handy place under which to hide some stolen packets of Dad's special fish formula!

'I knew it!' bellowed Dad.

'Stop her!' screeched Mum.

But Donna was too quick for them. She turned and started to leg it down the path, surprisingly fast for somebody wearing twelve-centimetre stiletto shoes.

Bill, unconcerned as ever by the lengths to

which we had gone to rescue him, had wandered round to the other side of the aquarium for a private chat with Kylie about the digger that was parked there. But when he saw Donna scampering off, he had one of his moments of genius.

'Quick, Dad! Take the digger! The keys are in the ignition!'

Dad didn't need telling twice. He jumped into the cab and the machine roared into life. Dad gave chase, with everybody, except Joe Blagg, running along behind.

As he caught up with Donna Mezzweme, he lowered the digger's bucket, leant out of the window and shouted, 'You're in a mess, Ms Mezz. I advise you to give yourself up! Otherwise I am going to scoop you up in this bucket and put you in the water with Kylie.' Dad laughed. 'And, between you and me, I don't think she's your biggest fan! In fact, I have it on good authority …' and he turned and winked at Bill, 'that she thinks you're rather dull!'

This was too much for Donna. '*DULL!* ME?' she screeched angrily. She stopped dead in her tracks, swung round – and stumbled into Dad's perfectly poised bucket.

'Hah! Gotcha!' said Dad triumphantly. And raising

the bucket into the air, he turned round, drove back
to the aquarium and tipped Ms Mezzweme straight
into the water with Kylie.

Donna was beside herself with rage. But she

couldn't protest as Kylie, thrilled to have this chance for revenge, chased her round and round the aquarium, biffing Donna's bottom with her nose and forcing her to swim faster and faster. Finally, exhausted and spent, Donna begged for mercy.

'Help me!' she begged, trying to avoid Kylie. 'Get me out of here!'

'Only if you say please,' said Mum, who's a great stickler for manners.

Donna glowered and ground her teeth. 'All right then, help me, *PLEASE!*' she muttered.

'Fair enough,' said Mum, taking out a notebook. 'We'll get you out of there, but *only* if you promise to do the following things.

'First: you must give back every single packet of Dan's fish food.'

Wet and defeated, Donna Mezzweme nodded her head.

'Second: you are going to write to the zoo and say that you have resigned and that Dan is to have your job as well as supplying Kylie with food. I also think you should give some of that money that I can see poking out of your handbag …' she pointed to a large canvas carrier that Donna had dropped on the ground, 'to the zoo so that they can make this horrible aquarium more fun for Kylie! After all, it's not only got to look good, it's got to feel good, too! By the way, you told everyone that you had lost every penny you had betting against Ned — so I can only suppose that you've filched that money from the till!'

Donna glared at mum and clutched her hands to her chest. 'Never!' she spat.

But Mum reached for Stacey's mobile phone and started to ring the police. Donna knew when she was beaten. She nodded crossly and sniffed.

'Can I get out now?' she asked grumpily.

Mum shook her head, putting her phone away. She still hadn't finished.

'And thirdly,' she continued, 'you are going to recommend that Joe Blagg is employed here every weekend. After all,' she reasoned, 'if he's busy here, he won't be able to bully anyone — *and* he'll be able to earn back all his parents' holiday money that he lost by betting that Ned wouldn't win the quiz!

'Then you are going to go to the airport and you are to get on an aeroplane to anywhere you want to go and you are never, ever to come back or try, ever again, to steal Dan's fish food or any of his other inventions. Nor are you going to tell anyone what has happened, or I'll make sure that Kylie (or one of her friends) comes and eats you for breakfast. Do I have your word?'

Looking as sour as a pickled herring, Donna Mezzweme agreed to all Mum's demands. Mum wrote the points down on a piece of paper and Donna signed it – plus a declaration that she had done it of her own free will. Then, and only then, did Dad, Mum, Stacey, Bill and I haul her out of the water and lead her towards her clapped-out car.

'Where are you going to go?' I asked her, watching Dad collect all his missing packets of Super-Strong Fish Crisps for Scarce Sea Fish and put them with the others by the wall of the aquarium.

Donna, putting on her wig and regaining her confidence by the second, sniffed. 'Hollywood!' she announced immediately. 'I am fed up with being an industrial spy and sneaking around the place like a thief! From now on, I'm going to give up my life of crime! I have a dream! *I* am destined for better things than this poxy zoo with its pathetic duck pond – I am destined to be a star!' But at that moment she tripped over her bag and broke the heels of her shoes. In her stockinged feet, she looked quite small.

Soon, Donna Mezzweme was gone. We would never see her again. Now all we needed to do was deal with Joe. We found him, damp and surly, but true to form – eating.

Joe had ignored everything that had been going on. Instead, he had been chomping his way through Dad's remaining special fish crisps. There wasn't a single packet left.

Joe was going to turn into a fish.

And there was nothing we could do to help change him back.

It was not a pleasant sight.

First Joe went green, then yellow and then red. Then he blew up like a big balloon. His shoulders rose up to his neck, his knees dropped down to his ankles.

He had turned into the biggest, ugliest bloater fish the world had ever seen.

'AAGH!' shouted Mum.

'AAGH!' Stacey and I yelled.

'Yippee!' croaked Kylie (or so Bill translated for me later). 'A toy!'

And that is almost the end of this fishy tale. Joe dived into the pool and didn't come out for almost three weeks. Soon, he was Kylie's best friend. As he explained later, he had always hated school and any kind of work. He was much happier here, showing off to an audience, safe in the knowledge that he was the biggest and ugliest fish in the world.

Nor did Joe's parents seem to mind — or at least not after Dad had explained everything to them very carefully several times. Once they realised that Joe was only suffering from a temporary condition, they actually looked rather relieved. Removed from their son's evil influence, they decided to give up their life of crime and open a pooch parlour instead. Together, they groomed the pets of the rich and famous. Their modern and dramatic hairstyles — specialities, 'The Afghan Elvis' and the 'Punk Rock Poodle' — were photographed worldwide.

And so, it seemed everyone was happy. Dad ran the aquarium, Kylie had a friend and Bill was the star turn: the boy who swam with the whale. And by the time

Joe finally turned back into a boy, guess what? He was a changed character (well, almost) – and the school's strongest swimmer. He won all the championships for miles around and when he wasn't busy ploughing up and down the local swimming pools, he spent the rest of his free time helping to look after the other animals at the zoo. Even if he had wanted to bully anyone, he simply did not have the time.

And as for those terrible T-shirts: do you know, we managed to shift every single one, just as Grotty Geoff had predicted? Thanks to the newspaper coverage of the school quiz, Dad managed to sell all the remaining 19,776 of them. They became that season's must-have fashion item – and Dad, with the help of the head teacher, used some of the profits to pay back everyone (with the exception of Joe Blagg and Donna Mezzweme) who had bet against me. As for Grotty Geoff the printer, he became the most talked-about man in town.

And me? I was well pleased. Not only had we managed to save Bill and defeat the local bully, I had actually won the TOL3, the PlayStation, the plasma TV *and* the surround-sound cinema in the quiz. Mum and Dad were dead cool about it all and let me keep every single bit – though I had to swap rooms with Stacey again as they didn't want it in the living room. Stacey didn't mind, though. She was allowed to redecorate her old one in whatever colours she wanted – though why she decided on bright pink and lime green baffles me … So everyone was happy, everything was fine … though I must confess a tiny secret …

I *still* cannot look at a fish without
checking if it really is a fish …
or just my brother Bill in disguise.

FIN